ALSO BY LOUISE ERDRICH

FOR CHILDREN

Grandmother's Pigeon
ILLUSTRATED BY JIM LAMARCHE

The Range Eternal
ILLUSTRATED BY STEVE JOHNSON AND LOU FANCHER

The Birchbark House
The Game of Silence
The Porcupine Year

NOVELS AND STORIES

Love Medicine
The Beet Queen
Tracks
The Bingo Palace
Tales of Burning Love
The Antelope Wife
The Last Report on the Miracles at Little No Horse
The Master Butchers Singing Club
Four Souls
The Painted Drum
The Plague of Doves
The Red Convertible
Shadow Tag
The Round House

POETRY

Jacklight
Baptism of Desire
Original Fire

NONFICTION

The Blue Jay's Dance
Books and Islands in Ojibwe Country

LOUISE ERDRICH

CHICKADEE

HARPER

An Imprint of HarperCollins*Publishers*

Library of Congress Cataloging-in-Publication Data

Erdrich, Louise.

Chickadee / Louise Erdrich. — 1st ed.

p.   cm.

Summary: Continuing the series that began with The
Birchbark House, The Game of Silence, and The Porcupine
Year, Chickadee follows a brand-new character, Omakayas's
son Chickadee. Kidnapped by two ne'er-do-well brothers
from his own tribe, Chickadee must make a daring escape,
forge unlikely friendships, and set out on the most exciting
and dangerous journey he's ever taken to get back home.

ISBN 978-0-06-057790-2 (trade bdg.)

ISBN 978-0-06-057791-9 (lib. bdg.)

I. Ojibwa Indians—Juvenile fiction. 2. Metis—Juvenile
fiction. [1. Ojibwa Indians—Fiction. 2. Metis—
Fiction. 3. Indians of North America—Superior, Lake,
Region—Fiction. 4. Indians of North America—Great
Plains—Fiction. 5. Kidnapping—Fiction. 6. Voyages and
travels—Fiction. 7. Family life—Fiction. 8. Superior, Lake,
Region—History—19th century—Fiction. 9. Great Plains—
History—19th century—Fiction.] I. Title.

PZ7.E72554Ch 2012   2012006565

[Fic]—dc23   CIP

                                                                    AC

Typography by Andrea Vandergrift

12 13 14 15 16 LP/RRDH 10 9 8 7 6 5 4 3 2 1

❖

First Edition

CONTENTS

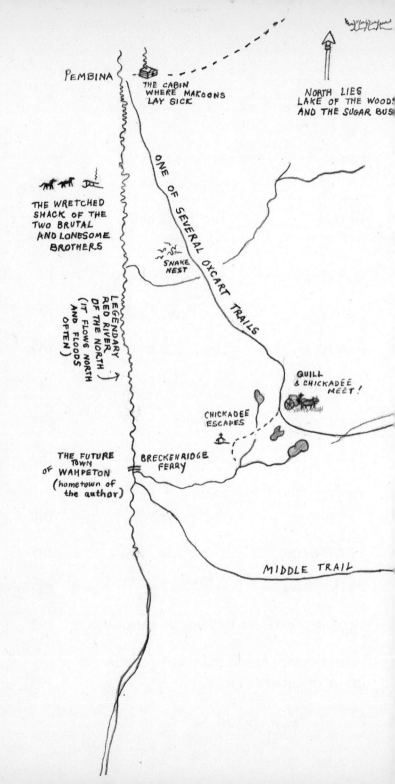

PEMBINA

THE CABIN WHERE MAKOONS LAY SICK

NORTH LIES
LAKE OF THE WOODS
AND THE SUGAR BUS

ONE OF SEVERAL OXCART TRAILS

THE WRETCHED
SHACK OF THE
TWO BRUTAL
AND LONESOME
BROTHERS

SNAKE
NEST

LEGENDARY
RED RIVER
OF THE NORTH
(IT FLOWS NORTH
AND FLOODS
OFTEN)

QUILL
& CHICKADEE
MEET!

CHICKADEE
ESCAPES

THE FUTURE
TOWN
OF WAHPETON
(hometown of
the author)

BRECKENRIDGE
FERRY

MIDDLE TRAIL

THE TRAIL OF OXCARTS
AND OF EVENTS WHICH
LED OUR FAMILY FROM
THE WOODS TO THE
GREAT PLAINS in a year
c. 1866
the chickadee taught his
namesake: small things
have great power

← THE GREAT MISSISSIPPI RIVER
WHICH BEGINS AS A TINY
STREAM, PROVING THE
TEACHING OF THE
CHICKADEE

WOODS TRAIL

MISSISSIPPI RIVER

METIS
FIDDLING & DANCING

MANSION ROW

SUMMIT AVENUE

ST. PAUL

HOMELAND OF THE
DAKOTA PEOPLE →

PROLOGUE

The year was 1866, and the girl whose first step was a hop, Omakayas, sometimes skipped as she chased after her children. Omakayas and her husband, Animikiins, had moved away from the villages on the shores of Lake of the Woods. They wanted to escape the illnesses that the fur traders brought along with bright cloth and wonderful tools. Omakayas, Animikiins, and their family lived in a remote land that gave them everything they needed: birchbark for making houses, animals and plants for food, wood for warmth, and cold sparkling water to dip and drink from the lake. This year, however, a most precious being would be stolen from them. They would follow. Only an act so shocking would bring them away from all they knew, onto the Great Plains. There they would learn how to survive in a landscape of harsh charms and brutal winds. They would learn the ways of the horse, the oxcart, and their new neighbors, the Metis. They would build their life anew and change forever.

ONE

THE HUNTING SPIRIT

Chickadee was sure that he remembered everything about the day that he and his twin brother were born.

"It was cold, wasn't it, Nimama? Just like today? Didn't the snow come suddenly? I remember that there was lots of snow!"

Omakayas looked down at him and smiled wearily. She had told this story a hundred times, and Chickadee had told it a hundred times more. He had heard it so many times that he now believed that *he* was the one who remembered every detail. He was an exhausting child, and there were two of him! His twin, Makoons, was using a stick to spear an imaginary bear like the old woman in his mother's stories.

"I'm Old Tallow!" he cried. "Stand still, Nimama. You be the bear!"

Omakayas growled and took the stick.

The twins were eight years old, and Omakayas was alone in the camp with them. Their father, Animikiins, was out hunting moose. Ordinarily, he would have taken the boys along so they could learn to hunt by his side. But today the air had that iron edge of snow. The sky was growing dark and the clouds looked heavy. Snow for certain. Perhaps that was why Chickadee could not stop talking about the day he was born.

"I remember," he started again, "you were out collecting wood. I was cold."

"*We* were cold," Makoons corrected.

"You were out collecting wood for a big fire, Nimama, when suddenly the snow just whirled down out of nowhere! It was a flash storm, a blizzard! You started back to the lodge. You staggered, carrying your load of wood."

Chickadee pitched forward and Makoons pretended he was a heavy wind and tried to push his brother over. Omakayas sighed again, and picked through some manoomin, wild rice, for stray stones and husks. She was boiling the last of their meat over a small fire and hoping that Animikiins would have luck out on the trail of a moose. She was humming a hunting song under her breath, to help him. Chickadee tugged on her heavy blue wool dress.

"You staggered into the camp! You barely made it! You crawled into the lodge and got close to the fire. You threw down the firewood and opened your blanket and—"

"Ai'ii," said Omakayas.

"There I was," said Chickadee, with great satisfaction. "I had come to help you. I had flown into your blanket."

"The snow was so thick in the air that the little chickadee must have knocked right into me, and nestled close," said Omakayas. She was always drawn into the story, in spite of herself.

"It was Iskigamizige-giizis, the Moon of Maple Sap, when we always get together to make maple sugar. There you were, in the sugaring camp. The chickadee had got whirled around in the snow, just like you!"

"And we came early, too," said Makoons. "We surprised you. We were very tiny. Each of us fit in a small makak, a little bowl. Our father could hold each of us in the palm of his hand."

"Eya'," said Omakayas, remembering what her grandmother, Nokomis, had said about how the world was created by twin brothers. As she had looked at the tiny babies that day, she wondered: Could they have been as small and helpless as these ones?

"The chickadee stayed with you the whole time we were getting born—that's why you named me for him, right?"

Omakayas thought of how the chickadee, unafraid, had perched near her the entire time. She smiled and nodded.

"And it was the time when little bears are born. They

were waking in their dens. It was a late snowstorm," said Makoons, whose name meant Little Bear.

"And nobody thought we would survive," both twins said with satisfaction. "Everybody said we would die."

Omakayas tried to hide the tears in her eyes.

"But you had strong guardian spirits," she said, remembering too. "The chickadee, the bear. Both there in the snow. They stayed near and helped us all."

At that moment, the twins' father, Animikiins, could have used some help. He had tracked a moose deep into a low mash-kiig, a wet marshland, and with every step his feet sank deep in freezing mushy grass. His feet were past pain and growing numb. But, like all Anishinabeg, he knew exactly where the line was between a numbness that could awaken painfully and a bitter, frozen numbness that meant the destruction of a foot or finger. He still had far to go, he thought, and took one careful step after another on the precarious ice. The moose was a large suspicious male with a heavy rack of antlers. It paused whenever Animikiins moved, ready to bolt, knowing something was not quite right.

The two moved farther, farther, out onto the spring-melted ice. The man and the moose stood motionless for what seemed an eternity to the man, but didn't bother the moose one bit. Then all of a sudden the moose gave a moose shrug and relaxed its guard. At that moment, Animikiins slowly raised his gun, fired, and, in taking a step forward, plunged into icy water up to his armpits. The moose turned, saw the man go down. Its eyes went red, its expression turned brutal as pain shot through its body, and it charged toward the man trying desperately to scramble back onto solid ice.

Back at home, the twins were still pestering their mother.

"Show us how you kept the blankets warm with rocks," said Makoons, "so we wouldn't die!"

"I've shown you that a hundred on a hundred times," said Omakayas. "Your father helped. He kept the flat stones from getting too hot. He got the stones to exactly the right temperature. Then we put your little sleeping makakoon on top of the rocks so you would stay warm. But mostly, I just carried you everywhere. You were so tiny I could hardly feel your weight."

"Now look at us," said Chickadee. "We are warriors."

"Warriors," laughed Omakayas. She smiled at her thin little boy whose spirit was so much larger than his body. "Yes, great warriors!" she said. "So how about checking my rabbit snares? How about doing a little hunting, too? And where is your father?"

Animikiins was trying to scrabble back onto frail ice. He raked at it with frozen hands. He'd thrown off his mitts. He kicked up once and fell back. The moose scrambled up the shore and ran off. At least now if he made it out of the freezing water, he wouldn't be stomped to death!

Animikiins kicked himself upward again, but slid backward, off the ice again, and cried out for help. The cry was loud, from the depth of his being. A hunting song came floating into his mind. He heard his love, his wife, Omakayas, singing. Her song gave him heart, but still he could feel a numb weakness spreading through him. What would his family do without him? He cried out once more. Then he saw something strange.

Animikiins saw his father standing on the shore. But that could not be! His father had died eight years ago. His father had always dressed in poor and ragged clothing, but now he wore a new blanket.

The blanket was not of this world—it was covered in

strokes of pale lightning. His father's head was covered with a beautiful woven turban. An eagle feather floated from the side. Oh, how kindly his eyes shone down.

"Deydey!" cried Animikiins.

He knew at that moment that his father had come to bring him to the spirit world.

"We're going, we're going!"

The boys laughed as Omakayas shooed them out the door. They ran into the woods with their small, strong bows and their quivers of arrows. During the winter, the fat partridges, binewag, liked to roost on low tree branches. Chickadee knew that his mother would smile with pride if he shot a bine from a tree branch. Zozie, who lived with them and was like his big sister, would happily pluck and roast it. She would tell him what a little man he was and stir some of the last maple sugar into the strengthening cedar tea that she would make for him.

"Bizindaan!" said Makoons. He stopped and looked around.

"What?" asked Chickadee.

"I thought I heard Father call," said Makoons.

"I don't hear anything," said Chickadee. "Nashke!" He pointed up at a tree where a fat and fluffy bine sat blinking its mild eyes. The boys crept to the exact right place to shoot. They silently fit their stone-tipped bird arrows to their bows. They both shot at once, but neither hit the bird. The bine just watched the arrows float by. It turned its head a little, ruffled its feathers.

Again, the boys brought up their bows. Again, they shot. And again, they missed.

The bine looked bored and shut its eyes for a nap.

Each of them had only two arrows, and now they had to go find them in order to shoot at the bird again. They were certain to scare the bine off, they thought. Knowing that they'd lost their chance, they walked boldly to the tree and thrashed around to find the arrows. To their surprise, the bird did not move.

"Maybe it knows how hungry we are," said Chickadee.

"Maybe our namesakes are helping us," said Makoons. "Although my little bear cubs are still sleeping this winter."

"Maybe our grandfathers are helping us from a distance," Chickadee said.

Again, they stood close to the perching bird, who looked even juicier now than before. Again they fit their arrows to their bows.

TWO

GAAWIIN MASHI

As his father smiled, Animikiins felt joy at seeing him, but also despair.

"Deydey," he gasped, gripping the ice, weakening, "I am not ready to die! Gaawiin mashi! Not yet!"

His father looked at him with steady eyes. Animikiins thought he was going to tell him, gently, to come along, just as he had when he was a boy. His father would tell him to come along to a place that frightened him, and he would join his father in the spirit world. But Animikiins did not want to go.

"I must go back!" he cried. "Father, I cannot join you!"

At last his father lowered his head and nodded. Then he pointed at a place on the ice just to the left of Animikiins. Suddenly Animikiins saw that a branch had lodged there, in the ice, a little beyond his grasp. But if he just kicked a

11

little harder, strained a bit more, he might reach it. Might reach it . . . there! With an effort he didn't think he was capable of, Animikiins pulled himself forward. Then he crawled and wiggled carefully across the thin ice onto the shore and stood. Where his father had been there was only empty snow. No tracks. Nothing.

Quickly, with numb hands but with an expert's knowledge that he had practiced since he was a child, Animikiins gathered dry birch shavings, moss, and bits of twigs. He had no feeling in his hands now, but he told them what to do, how to hold the striker, the steel, how to cup the spark and steadily breathe an ember to life in a tiny nest of kindling. In no time, Animikiins had a fire going in the spot where his father had appeared to him. He dried out his mitts, which had been strung inside his jacket. He winced as the blood entered his fingers and his toes. They'd throb and ache for days after this. But he was alive.

"Miigwech, indeydey," he said. "Miigwech for your love. Thank you for giving me this good life."

Twice more the twins shot and missed the bine, and yet it still waited in the tree. The bird's patience was beginning to spook the boys.

"Do you think it is a spirit bird?" asked Chickadee.

"Maybe it just wants us to eat," said Makoons. With a gasp he released his arrow, and the bird fell from the tree.

"Wait," said Chickadee. "Your arrow didn't hit the bine!

I saw your arrow hit the tree! This is definitely a ghost bird and I don't want to go near it."

"Ah, the great warriors," laughed a girl behind them.

"Zozie!"

She had two more rocks in her hand. It was Zozie who had brought the bird down into the snow.

"Did you check the snares?"

The twins shook their heads, and she smiled down at them. Zozie was tall and pretty. They were bashful and a little bit in love with her. She was the daughter of their mother's powerful, enigmatic, bold, and sometimes blood-thirsty cousin, Two Strike. Zozie loved her mother, but as Two Strike readily admitted, her heart really wasn't in mothering. Two Strike loved to hunt and was far off to the north on a trapline. Zozie was happy to stay with Omakayas, who loved her and called her daughter.

"Waabooz," she cried now, catching sight of a trapped rabbit. They knelt near a snare and removed the frozen rabbit. There was another rabbit caught in a snare set farther on. That one had already been half eaten by a weasel.

"Tracks," said Chickadee. "We just missed the weasel. I would have shot it."

"No, I would have shot it," said Makoons.

"Just like you shot the partridge?" asked Zozie.

The twins scuffled their feet in the snow, looked down, and didn't answer.

• • •

13

After he felt the chill leave his heart, and after he got used to the fact that he would live, Animikiins remembered that his family was very hungry. His empty-handed return would disappoint them. Oh, they would cry when he told them about seeing his father. Omakayas would hold his hands to her face. The boys would cling to him. Zozie would hang her head and sigh. But they would all be even hungrier than they had been when he'd left. As a hunter, that made him very angry. Animikiins jumped to his feet.

Where had that moose gone, the moose that drove him into the lake and nearly cost him his life? It had surged up the shore just past the spot where Animikiins's father had appeared. It had not looked back, but melted away into a heavy stand of spruce. Animikiins followed. All of a sudden he stopped. A splash of dark blood lit the snow, then another and another. A bit farther on he saw the dark mound of the moose. Animikiins looked into the sky and smiled. He thanked his father just as the first flakes, and more flakes, and then a thin cloth and then at last a heavy blanket of snow began to fall.

And fall. And fall.

THREE

REUNION

Zozie breathed the deeply cold air and smelled snow coming.

"Giigawedaa," she said. "Let's go home." The boys trudged behind her, each carrying a rabbit. She had the partridge. Omakayas would be very, very glad to see them. On the way back, Zozie sang a little traveling song and the boys sang too. Each beat of the song was a footstep, and even when the snow began to fall they marched along cheerfully. They were sure that their father would make it home before them, and that if he'd had no luck he would be filled with praise for their skills.

By the time they reached the camp, the snow was

swirling through the air. The wind was blowing hard and groaning in the trees. They could hardly see their birch-bark house, their wigwassi-wigamig, but they heard the dog barking. A crack of warm light showed through the blanket slung over the entry, and Omakayas parted the door and came outside.

"Is Deydey back yet?"

"Gaawiin mashi," said Omakayas.

"Look at what we brought! What great hunters we are!" The twins gave their rabbits excitedly to Omakayas, forgetting that she was the one who had set the snares.

"Howah! And this plump bine, too! Did my little men hunt this bird?" Omakayas smiled at her twins, who looked up at Zozie.

"We tried!" said Chickadee.

"Zozie knocked it down with a rock," said Makoons.

Omakayas laughed and brushed the snow from Zozie's hair.

"Her mama was always a deadly aim with a rock, too!" Omakayas was remembering the sting of Two Strike's pebbles when her cousin was angry, but that was long ago.

Zozie smiled, but looked around anxiously and said, "My uncle is not back."

"He can take good care of himself," said Omakayas.

But everyone noticed that, when Omakayas made the stew that night and dished it out, she put a little makak out for the spirits and a full bowl on the mat with the other food. That bowl was for Animikiins. No one touched it, but they all watched the bowl as the steam rose from the delicious meat and then, slowly, cooled.

The snow came down so suddenly that Animikiins knew that he was trapped. He was far from the camp. He didn't dare walk so far in a disorienting blizzard, even to bring meat to his family. No, he had to camp where he was. And he'd better seek shelter fast. Luckily, he was in heavy spruce, and spruce branches could be made into a lean-to. He broke off an armload of boughs, took a hatchet to some larger branches, and quickly built himself a lean-to. He set it against a great rock, only a few feet from the place where the moose had died. With the snow falling thickly, there was no possibility of building a fire. Animikiins heaped snow into a circle, high as he could. The snow was good insulation. He would sleep on a bed of boughs with thicker boughs to cover himself. At last, just before he nestled into a shelter as wind tight as he could make it, Animikiins drew his knife and sliced out the moose's tongue and liver. He brought both into the shelter, heaped snow against the opening, and ate a bloody, raw, satisfying meal before he dozed off to sleep.

• • •

One day. Two days. Three days of snow. The first night, the little family ate half the pot of stew. The second night, they ate the rest of the kettle and scraped the bottom with a knife. The third night, with great misgivings, they divided and ate the bowl of stew that had been sitting by the fire for Animikiins. Then they fell asleep. It wasn't much, and their insides gnawed.

Halfway through the night, Omakayas woke, restless. Outside the snow drove down and the wind still growled and shook the branches of the trees. The snow was heaping higher and higher around the entrance of the wigwam. The dog, who had chewed up and devoured the already gnawed bones of the rabbits, was curled at the door with his tail over his head. It was still snowing, but Omakayas thought she heard something, someone. She shivered as a trickle of fear went up her back.

Sometimes when the trees cracked and the snow came

down hard, the spirit of winter, Biboonang, was out walking. It was a harsh spirit, and Omakayas didn't want to challenge it. She crept from her blankets and built up the fire. They would have to find some food tomorrow.

The day dawned bright, the snow was finished. Although the air was hard and cold the twins were elated to walk out on top of the drifts. There was no knowing where Animikiins had gone to, but Omakayas decided to set out after him anyway. She put on her snowshoes, took the dog with her, and told the twins and Zozie to set new snares and to gather balsam and melt snow for hot tea when she got home. She pulled a toboggan behind her and had a keen hatchet in her belt, which was lucky, for she hadn't been walking half an hour when Animikiins hailed her.

"Ahneen," she yelled with happiness.

They hurled themselves together and held close. They had known each other since they were children, and they treasured each other very deeply. They swore that they had known they would be married ever since Omakayas had given food to the hungry boy who would become her husband.

Animikiins had glared at her, starving, on that day so long ago, but her gift of food had eventually melted his glare, and his heart, too.

Now Omakayas rejoiced. They had real food. A moose

would last them the rest of the winter. Piece by piece, the family hauled back the moose using the toboggan. Everyone also carried chunks of frozen meat with carrying straps. By the time they cached the meat near their camp, hoisting some into a tree, burying some in snow, they were warm and excited.

Omakayas brought in the tenderest pieces of meat and began to make a feast. The rest of the family had been hunting in the next bay. Now they gathered.

Mikwam, Ice, was Omakayas's father. She called him Deydey. Yellow Kettle was her mother. But nobody called her grandmother yet because Nokomis, Grandmother, was still alive and strong. Old as she was, Nokomis kept up with Mikwam and joked that when she smelled the meat roasting she'd come running and leave him behind on the trail.

There was Omakayas's beautiful sister, Angeline, and her husband, Fishtail. Angeline had survived a terrible illness, smallpox. She had no children, and this made her sad except when Zozie came to live with her. Zozie called three different women Nimama, and nobody thought that strange.

The whole family gathered that night. The wigwam was crowded and noisy, and everyone ate and told stories late into the night. Chickadee and Makoons curled together under one fluffy rabbit-skin blanket. Warm and full, lulled by the grown-ups' voices, they fell into a charmed sleep and dreamed, as they always did, together.

FOUR

SMALL THINGS

Winter and spring went back and forth that year. Nokomis said that the spirit of winter was struggling harder than usual to keep his claws of ice on the world. Still, the maple sap began to run one warm day, and the family was ready. They had already made camp at the same great stand of sugar maples where the twins were born.

Chickadee watched his namesake hop from twig to twig in the branches of the sugar maples. He had managed to sneak away from the close watch of his mother. He had evaded his father, ditched his grandmother. He had hidden from his aunt, his uncle, his grandfather, and even

his twin. There was nobody to tell him to keep hauling sap
from the trees.

"Haul sap! Haul sap! More sap!"

But the real reason he'd snuck away was
that he'd heard the old man Zhigaag laughing at him. Every year Zhigaag came to sugar,
sometimes bringing his brutish sons. Zhigaag watched everyone work, but did nothing himself. He just complained until
someone gave him sugar to quiet him, and every year the old
man's taunts and jeers grew worse.

"Look at that weakling! He's scrawny like his namesake!"

Chickadee's face burned with shame when he heard
that, and he stumbled. He spilled some sap from the
makak he was carrying. The old man gave a mean laugh.
Chickadee had hauled makak after makak of sap from the
taps in the trees to the great boiling kettles, taking care
every time not to splash himself or spill. Now the mean
remark made him clumsy with embarrassment.

He had done nothing wrong, he thought with fury. Of
course, every so often he had paused to drink the strengthening and delicious, faintly sweet sap, but everyone did
that. Sap was a spring tonic. He'd been a good worker and
did not deserve the old man's comment.

So he'd sneaked away.

Couldn't a boy have some respect? And a minute or two
for rest? Couldn't a boy have a little while to lie in last year's
newly warmed, fragrant maple leaves? Couldn't a boy spend

a little time gazing into the swaying tops of the maples?

Chickadee's thoughts turned darker. He didn't really mind the work. It was that mean old John Zhigaag whom he wanted to get away from. A fitting name for a cranky old person—John Skunk. It was Zhigaag who called him scrawny, Zhigaag who picked on young boys with his nasty temper, ruining the good time they had running wild and sneaking bits of sugar or bannock or the choicest bits of meat. Zhigaag was always there to point them out, to catch them at their tricks, to scream out, "There they go, catch them!"

Yes, it was Zhigaag who embarrassed him, Zhigaag who always got them in trouble. Even worse, the old man had those two powerful sons who enjoyed trouble just as much as their father.

But for a moment, Chickadee was hidden from the old man's eyes, and everybody else's eyes, behind a small hillock of stone. And there he continued watching his namesake. The chickadee had begun its spring song, which

was a sweet and lilting song, not the mischievous scolding of winter. Every spring when this happened, Chickadee felt a wash of happiness come over him. It was a promise of warmth, food, berries, summer, swimming, and fun. But this time, as he listened, he heard old Zhigaag's words.

"Scrawny? Am I scrawny? Are you a weakling, my namesake?"

As he watched his tiny namesake hop from twig to twig, Chickadee felt disappointed for the first time. Why couldn't he have a protector like the bear or the lynx or the caribou or  the eagle? Why was he singled out by such an insignificant little bird? He had a sudden thought that appalled him—he would be a grown man and still be called Chickadee! What kind of name was that for a powerful warrior? He groaned.

"Oh, my namesake, why did you choose me?"

Suddenly, the little bird flew away. Chickadee turned over and closed his eyes. He sensed the great strong roots of the maple trees drawing water from the earth and sweetening it with their own sugar. He should have felt joy. But he was laughed at, overworked, unappreciated, and deserted even by his namesake. His eyes stung with pity for himself.

"Ah, there you are!"

Chickadee sighed and sat up, brushed the leaves from

his hair. At least it wasn't old Zhigaag who'd found him.

It was Nokomis, which was not so bad. She was very good at getting around with her little walking stick, and she never told him what to do. His great-grandmother was so old that she had dim eyesight, though, uncannily, she never mistook him for his twin, the way other people did. She put her hand in her little buckskin bag for a treat.

"Did I give you your sugar lump, my boy?"

"Oh, no, my Nookoo, not yet!" Chickadee hid the sugar lump he already had in his cheek and put out his hand.

"You are a good boy," said Nookoo. "But you can't fool me, Chickadee. I'll give you extra anyway. And here, give this other lump to your brother. What are you doing here? This is my secret place!"

Chickadee was amazed that his great-grandmother, who tottered around and couldn't see or hear very well anymore, had noticed his lumpy cheek, and more, that she had a secret place. Why would she need a secret place?

"I used to come here when I was a little girl," said Nookoo, settling herself against the rock. "We Anishinabeg have been coming here since time began. Did you know that these trees are the children of the original spirit trees who understood us and told us how to gather their water and boil it into syrup and sugar so long ago?"

"Gaawiin, Nookoo!"

Chickadee was more curious than most boys, who might have run off right after getting an extra treat.

"Why have you hidden yourself away?" Nokomis asked. Although she was ancient, his great-grandmother always saw into his heart.

Because she always listened to him, Chickadee always told her the truth.

"Old John Zhigaag said that I was scrawny, a weakling, just like my namesake."

"What!"

Great-Grandmother's eyes filled with a cloudy fire. Her back straightened. She thumped her walking stick on the ground.

"This is very bad, my boy, very bad!" she cried. "Doesn't the old fool realize that you must never insult the chickadee?"

"Oh?"

Chickadee remembered that he himself had been disrespectful to the little bird, and that it had flown away. Uneasily, he scratched his head and sat closer to Nookoo.

"Why is it you must never insult the chickadee?" he asked in a low voice.

His great-grandmother gave him a surprised look. "Don't you know? Haven't you realized yet? Small things have great power."

Chickadee was struck by this. He sat back on his heels. *Small things have great power* sounded good, but made no sense.

"But I am scrawny. I am a weakling. And the chickadee is little too. It has no teeth, no claws. What can it do?"

"The chickadee stays awake all winter in the cold," said Nokomis. "He survives on the smallest seeds. He is a teacher. The chickadee shows the Anishinabeg how to live. For instance, he never stores his food all in one place. He makes caches in various places. He never eats all of his food at once. We do that too. The chickadee takes good care of his family. The mother and the father stay with their babies as they fly out into the world. They stick together, like the Anishinabeg. And there are other things. The chickadee is always cheerful even in adversity. He is brave and has great purpose, great meaning. You are lucky to have your name."

Chickadee put his hands on his face. "Lucky! Great-Grandmother, I insulted the chickadee! I told the bird he was a weakling. I asked why he had chosen me!"

Great-Grandmother now looked extremely grieved.

"What can I do?"

She rummaged in her carrying bag and took out three hazelnuts. Giving them to Chickadee, she said, "Crack these into small pieces and place them on this rock. I will put tobacco at the base of the rock. Then, we wait."

Chickadee followed her instructions, and just as she had said, they waited. The sun went behind a cloud. The shadows grew cold. The chickadee did not appear. Finally, Nokomis spoke out loud.

"Oh, chickadee. Please accept our offering! Your name-sake is young and had his feelings hurt. He did not wish to offend you. Please don't reject him! He needs your counsel!"

"I am very sorry," whispered Chickadee. "Please come back to me."

Now it seemed to him that all of his life he'd heard the chickadee's call near him. His namesake had always been around, looking after him. It was strange not to hear that voice, strange only to hear the distant cries of humans and other birds. A shadow fell across his heart.

"Where are you?" Chickadee whispered.

All of a sudden there was a swift motion, a small flutter, and the chickadee came down onto the rock. It did not peck up the nuts but stared intently at its namesake, then at Great-Grandmother. She stared back just as hard at the bird. They regarded each other for what seemed like the longest time to Chickadee. Then the bird decisively pecked up a bit of the hazelnut, and flew to a nearby twig. It held the nut against the twig with its small black claw, and ate it quickly. Then it flew right back for another piece.

"We can go now," said Nokomis, sighing in relief.

FIVE

SONS OF ZHIGAAG

As Chickadee and Nokomis walked back to join their family, they passed John Zhigaag sitting on a stump. He leaned on a long, thick stick. As the two passed, he stuck the stick out right in the path of Nokomis. He meant to trip her and his snaggle-toothed grin showed that he would enjoy see-ing her sprawl at his feet.

"Nookoo, watch out!" cried Chickadee. She stepped forward.

Crack!

Instead of tripping over the old man's walking stick, Nokomis used her own. Her walking stick came down on John Zhigaag's head, smashing down his lumpy, frayed, treasured top hat.

"Yow!"

The hat smashed down so hard that it ripped. Zhigaag's ears stuck out the fragile sides. The old man looked so comical that Nokomis and Chickadee couldn't help laughing. Once they started, and once John Zhigaag began to stamp and bray, they laughed even harder. They laughed so hard that tears came into their eyes. Old John Zhigaag raised his stick in the air and threatened to run them down. In his rage, he began to sputter and choke on his own fury. As Nokomis and Chickadee stumbled away, they had to hold their aching stomachs. They were still weeping with laughter when they reached the family camp. Nokomis sat down and tried to regain her breath.

"What is it? What happened?" Omakayas took her grandmother's hand, alarmed, and patted it anxiously.

Nokomis tried to speak, but every time she spoke the name of John Zhigaag she burst out laughing again. She pointed at Chickadee.

"He will tell you!" she cried.

So Chickadee told the story of how John Zhigaag

tried to trick Nokomis, and how she had known exactly how to use her stick even though she was half-blind. Chickadee described Zhigaag's hat and Omakayas could not help laughing too. That hat was Zhigaag's symbol of prestige.

Chickadee told his family how Zhigaag had tormented him that day, and how he'd gone off to hide. Makoons, especially, was immediately infuriated by the insults the old man had given to his brother.

"You're not a weakling! You're strong and bold, like me!"

The truth was that both twins, who had started out so tiny, had never grown as big and strong as most boys their age. John Zhigaag knew this, thought Omakayas when she heard the names he'd called Chickadee. But he should never have shamed her son. She was glad that Nokomis had given the old man a sore head and had ruined his pride and joy, his hat.

But even as Omakayas was thinking this, Makoons was thinking the same thing. He was thinking how unfair it was of Zhigaag to insult his brother, and how very bad it was that he tried to trip Nokomis on the path. She could have been hurt. It showed a lack of respect.

"There is only one way to make him respect us all," muttered Makoons. He slipped away. It was dusk and a slim boy could hide near the old man's shelter. There was still time to play one more trick on the old man, a trick that would make him leave Nokomis and Chickadee alone for good.

That night, while everyone was asleep, Makoons crept into Zhigaag's tiny bark shelter. First, he untied the old man's

dangling moccasin strings. He was sleeping in his moccasins, so this was a very difficult task. It took Makoons quite a while to undo the string. Then he had to wait while the old man snuffled and snorted and turned over in his sleep. Finally, he managed to tie the moccasins to each other. While he was doing this, he had another idea.

Makoons took a piece of loose birchbark off a tree. Then he slipped back to his family's camp and crept up to the fire, which was banked for the night and gave off just enough warmth for the family to sleep by.

"I'll be right back," said Makoons. With a stick, he reached into the pot and smeared a large lump of fat on the piece of birchbark. Makoons sneaked furtively and quickly back to Zhigaag's shelter, which rattled with his snores. He leaned in and smeared the back of the old man's jacket with the fat. Then Makoons went back to his own sleeping corner inside his family's wigwam and fell asleep in great satisfaction. He'd revenged his family, upheld his brother's honor, and he felt certain that John Zhigaag would have only the greatest respect for his grandmother from now on.

Late the next morning, at the time when John Zhigaag usually rose, there was a roar of hilarity from the end of the sugar camp. Makoons gave a sign to Chickadee, and both ran over to see what the excitement was about.

To their satisfaction, John Zhigaag was wiggling out of his shelter like an earthworm, with the hat pulled low over his ears. His ankles were bound together with his moccasin laces. As he appeared at the entrance, dozens of mice, which had been feasting on the fat that coated his jacket, jumped off and scurried away. The mice had eaten most of the fabric along with the fat, and when the strings were untangled and he was able to stand, the halves of his fancy coat fell abruptly off his arms. The mice had eaten the entire back away.

Now the whole camp howled with laughter. John Zhigaag had been mean to nearly everyone around him, and there were few who had much sympathy for him. But as he stamped and roared and swore he would get even, he woke his big angry sons, who had ridden up to the camp the day before on shaggy brown horses.

Whether or not these two hard-faced men had sympathy for their father was impossible to tell. They watched impassively as their father raved and swore at the pieces of his coat. They did not help him. But their cold narrow eyes passed over the other people one by one, and many of those who laughed fell silent.

These two sons, Babiche and Batiste, were silent, crafty, massive men who liked no one better than each other. They trusted only each other. Having been starved and beaten by their father in their youth, they came to his aid only for form's sake. They looked around the gathering to ascertain who had embarrassed their father, not because they loved him, but because they loved revenge.

A pall fell over everybody at the camp, and Nokomis stamped away muttering that the gathering would be ruined now. With these two hard men watching everything that took place, the ease and pleasure of the undertaking, the taste of sugar after a hard winter, and the sharing of the maples' gifts, would be spoiled, she said.

She had no idea that things would be worse, much worse, than that.

Later that day, as Chickadee and Makoons again hauled makak after makak of sap to the giant boiling kettles, they tried to avoid Zhigaag and his two sons. Luckily, their mother was engaged in the difficult but delightful task of making sugar. Both boys put down their makakoon and stayed near to help her, and help Nokomis, knowing that their reward would be a cone or two of sugar as a treat.

Omakayas knelt beside a maple log that Animikiins had scraped and smoothed into a sugaring trough. Nokomis ladled syrup, which had been boiled until it was so hot the surface crumpled like a thick skin, onto the heavy tray. Then the two women took turns working it back and forth with wooden paddles carved especially for this task.

This was very hard work—the women kept the paddles constantly in motion and stirred the syrup fast, fast, fast, until it magically crystalized into lovely, sandy-colored grains. But even though they were panting and their arms had begun to ache, both were smiling. The scent of the new sugar was so pleasant, and behind them the kettles of bubbling sap and hot fires exuded such a fine aroma. Birds fluttered and sang out high in the branches. The cool, fresh breeze came from Zhawanong, the South, the bringer of green life to the Anishinabe world.

A visitor sat watching them on a stump, asking questions from time to time. He spoke French or English, so Nokomis couldn't understand him. But Omakayas, who knew and understood the languages from listening to her father, answered the man in the black robe.

Mekadewikonayewinini. Black Robe.

That's what Omakayas called the curious man. Catholic priests were known as the black robes—they dressed in the same curious costumes and carried a certain book.

They sometimes pulled out anama'eminensag, or what some called praying berries or praying ropes. Their hands moved on these strings of beads as they recited the same words over and over. They were interesting people, and sometimes took the trouble to learn the Anishinabe language. This priest lived as the Anishinabe did, too, and traveled with those who had moved out onto the Plains. He was known to them all as Father Genin. This priest had come to the sugaring camp in order to learn about how the Ojibwe made their delicious sugar. This priest had traveled from the prairies past the Pembina Hills, with the two hard sons of Zhigaag. On the way, he'd hoped to convert them, but seeing as all the way there they'd fought, swore, hit their horses, drank whiskey, and insulted each other long into the night, it was evident that he had failed.

SIX

THE WAY IT HAPPENED

Chickadee and Makoons were taking a well-deserved rest. They were making sure they got their rest by hiding behind the rocks again. Slowly they licked the cones of sugar that Nokomis had given them.

"Brother," said Makoons in a worried voice, "how many family and friends do we have here?"

"Let's count," said Chickadee.

The twins tried to count everyone in their family. Some were missing though. Animikiins, Fishtail, and Two Strike were hunting.

"And how much family does Zhigaag have?" asked Makoons.

"Just his sons, but they're worth several warriors apiece."

"That worries me," said Makoons. "Because I am the one who tied the old man's moccasins together and made a feast for the mice out of his jacket. I had to take revenge for Nookoo, and for you, my brother."

"Miigwech, thank you," said Chickadee with a grin.

Chickadee was not surprised by his brother's confession. His twin was a clever joker, and this prank had worked all too well.

"I am just worried that I have got us all into trouble," said Makoons. "I wish that Two Strike, our Deydey, Fishtail, or even Uncle Quill was here. They could take on ten Zhigaags. I didn't know that Babiche and Batiste would show up."

"Did you see the way they looked at us?"

"No doubt they have their suspicions."

"I think Zhigaag told them about the problem with his hat," said Chickadee.

"His hat will never be the same. I wonder what he's wearing today—no fancy hat, no trader's topcoat."

The twins lay back against the rock and gazed into the waving tops of the maple trees. Lost in their silent thoughts, they did not notice the rustling of footsteps. Then suddenly there were voices, grown men's voices. Babiche and Batiste sat down on the rock. There was the scrape of a striker, and then the wafting odor of tobacco. As the two men puffed on their pipes, the twins shrank against the rock. They hardly breathed. Their hearts beat frantically. Makoons closed his eyes in fear, but Chickadee kept one eye open.

"One of those two scrawny puppies has shamed our father," Babiche said at last.

"We should catch them and throw them in the soup pot," said Batiste.

"Har, har, har," laughed Babiche. "They wouldn't make more than a few mouthfuls for men like us."

"Look down at my leg," said Batiste. "The muscles are so big I could outrun a horse."

"You are mighty, my brother," Babiche agreed. "But just look at my fist. It is so hard it could smash a rock."

"Your fist is hard," said Batiste. "And as large as your own head."

"Har, har, har," laughed Babiche. "You are very funny, my brother."

Makoons opened one eye and looked into Chickadee's open eye. The twins silently agreed that Babiche and Batiste weren't funny.

"Think," said Babiche, blowing out a cloud of smoke, "of what we could do to those worthless puppies with your leg, and my fist."

"Or my two fists, and your head."

"Or your two legs, and my one fist."

"Or if we squeezed them between our rock-hard bellies!"

"Har, har, har," laughed Babiche. "You are funny, my brother."

"All we need to do is get them alone, with nobody watching us."

Chickadee's and Makoon's eyes opened wide in alarm. Then they felt the two massive men moving above them, leaning over them, and they saw the craggy faces of the brothers very near. Suddenly both brothers sucked hard on their pipes and then blasted smoke out into the boys' eyes.

How it burned! Although blinded, the twins leaped up anyway, fast as rabbits. They jumped, fell, scurried, blundering into trees and tripping over branches as they fled.

Behind them, the powerful big brothers flexed the

muscles of their arms and compared their fists again, smoked their pipes, and laughed and laughed.

Chickadee and Makoons reeled back to the safety of their camp to find the women in the family were finishing their work. They crept into the wigwam to hide, hoping that the family would leave the camp very soon.

It seemed they would. Once the nights and the days were warm, and the sun increased its strength, the days of sugar bush were over. Omakayas wrapped the tawny blocks of maple sugar in birchbark and tied the bark down with split jack-pine root. After the sugaring, the family planned to return to the islands in the Lake of the Woods, where they would hunt furs and build their stores of food through the summer. They all looked forward to warm days of fishing, berry picking, gathering medicines, and swimming.

But the two sons of Zhigaag had something else in mind.

Even as the other families gathered their blankets and pots and prepared to move, Babiche and Batiste sat on the rock. There, the pipe smoke drifting up in curls, they hatched an inglorious plan.

"We are important," said one brother.

"That is true," said Batiste. "We carry the mail on our horses. Everyone treats us with respect."

"But our shanty, it is a mess," said Babiche. "I was thinking how nice it would be to have a wife."

"A wife is too much trouble," replied his brother. "Besides, we'd need two. We couldn't share a wife."

"Har, har," said Babiche, "you are funny, my brother. What we need is a servant."

"A servant! Now that is a fine idea. We are important enough to have a servant, but where would we get one?" asked Batiste.

"I have an idea," said Babiche. "Those two insulting rabbits who look exactly alike—what if one disappeared?"

"We might get in trouble with that whole family," said Batiste.

"Oh, I very much doubt it, my brother," said Babiche. "Remember, they have two the same! They have an extra! Why should they care?"

"Har. You are very funny! But perhaps you are also right."

Late that night, while the whole camp slept, the two men crept to the birchbark shelter where the twins dreamed of all they would do back on their island. With a stealth surprising for his size, Babiche wiggled his hands and arms underneath the loose walls. He seized the twin closest to him, put his rough hand over the boy's mouth, and yanked him so quickly out under the birchbark wall that the other sleepers were not stirred.

Ever since she was a young girl, Omakayas had been visited in her dreams by a protective spirit, a bear woman. That night, the furry and powerful bear woman appeared.

Omakayas dreamed that the bear woman crawled in beside her and curled up, speaking sleepily, for she was only now stirring from her winter hibernation.

"Omakayas, my child, your little ones are in danger. The hunters are coming. . . ."

Omakayas woke with a start and stirred up the fire just enough to see. There was Nokomis, curled in her rabbit-skin blanket. And there was Zozie sleeping flat on her back underneath a trade blanket. Makoons was a lump entirely wrapped in another blanket, and next to him there was a lump too. But something about the lump did not look right.

Omakayas stirred the little fire into flames, causing Nokomis to sit up, blinking.

"Chickadee?"

There was no answer.

Omakayas went over to Chickadee's blanket, felt around the spot, and noticed that the birchbark wall was pulled up. At first she thought he had gone out to the bushes. She waited. Nokomis turned over, went back to sleep. Chickadee did not return. Omakayas's heart jolted in fear. My bear woman has spoken the truth! She woke Makoons.

"Mama?" He rubbed his eyes.

"Where is your brother?"

Makoons leaned over the empty blanket and tried to focus his sleepy eyes.

"Dibi'. I don't know where!"

In an instant, Omakayas was out the door, hoping that

Chickadee had only slipped out on some midnight errand with a cousin. She went to every lodge, waking everyone. None of them had seen Chickadee.

Now the whole camp was out, including Zozie and Makoons. They called out for Chickadee. They made torches of pitch-tipped branches. Father Genin crawled out of his blankets and tried to help. Everyone searched the area. Everyone, that is, except Babiche and Batiste. John Zhigaag had crept out to poke his walking stick here and there in the leaves.

"Old Zhigaag! Where are your sons?" asked Nokomis.

"I don't know," said Zhigaag.

"You know something," said Nokomis. "Those two sons of yours have stolen Chickadee!"

"Stolen? Why, you couldn't give away that worthless boy," said the old man. "Nobody would want him!"

"Then where is he?" said Nokomis. "And where are Babiche and Batiste? Answer me!"

"My sons may have gone back to the river," replied Zhigaag. "They will catch some golden eyes when the river breaks up. They were hungry for golden eyes!"

"Hungry for fish in the middle of the night!"

Nokomis made ready to hit the old man again with her walking stick, but he threw himself on the ground and cried out, "Pity me! I have no one! My sons didn't even take me along!"

"Oh, you pity yourself enough," said Nokomis.

Father Genin came over and helped the old man sit up. "Where are your sons?"

He also was suspicious, especially since he'd failed to convert Babiche and Batiste. In spite of his forgiving nature, he suspected that they were unredeemable fellows and were even capable of wickedness. He made Zhigaag sit still and listen while he said a few quick prayers.

Nokomis hobbled quickly over to Omakayas, who was examining the sets of footprints outside the wigwam. The footprints led straight to where the two brown horses had been tethered. Omakayas fell down on her knees, grasping Deydey's hand.

"Oh, Deydey, they have stolen Chickadee!"

Deydey's face was suffused with fury.

"My daughter," he said, "we will pursue them. We will find our boy."

The twins were favorites of his, favorites of everyone. Everyone knew how, in the stories, twins helped to create the Ojibwe world. Twins were considered blessed. To know twins, to be in the family of twins or even the presence of twins, was good fortune. Chickadee and Makoons were much loved. To divide twins was an evil.

"I will track down Babiche and Batiste," said Mikwam. "Fishtail and Animikiins will follow the path as well. When Two Strike hears of this, she'll take it hard! We'll catch up with them. Don't worry, daughter."

In a gesture rare for him, Mikwam put his arm around Omakayas's shoulder and tried to comfort her weeping. She in turn held Makoons. Poor Makoons had never been separated from his brother, and he was crying with all of his heart. Nothing would be right for anyone until Chickadee returned.

SEVEN

THE CHASE

Chickadee's dream was frightening in the first place. It was a nightmare. A huge black flying turtle had chased him through trees and over rocks. Chickadee had been just about to wake when a smothering hand was clapped over his mouth and he was suddenly somewhere else. The last thing he saw was the tiny flare of light inside his family wigwam. Then nothing. All was darkness. He made sounds as he was hauled up, swung around, thumped down. But those sounds were no more than panicked whines. He was sure nobody heard him.

In all that was to come, he would fix on that little

moment he'd seen the flare of light. He would wish, and wish, that he'd bitten the hand of Babiche, or shoved a stick in the eye of Babiche. He wished he had awakened sooner, or managed to grab the feet of his brother, who would have shouted the alarm.

But everything happened swiftly, brutally. Now, tied in a sack, Chickadee was slung across a thick blanket on the back of a horse. He thought it was one of the brown horses that Babiche and Batiste had arrived on. They were galloping away before Chickadee could really make sense of things. It was all too fast, all too strange, all like part of the dream. It was as if the dream had come true and he was snatched into the air by the flying black turtle!

Chickadee was terrified, but as he was held tight against the woolly vest of Babiche, sitting on a comfortable blanket, and enveloped in a dark sack, he also began to get sleepy again.

I might as well sleep, thought Chickadee. *No sense worrying about things now. If I wiggle hard, I'll just fall off. I am certainly taken captive. If I sleep now, I'll be better able to handle what happens when this horse finally stops.*

As soon as Animikiins and Two Strike found out what had happened, they decided to start out. The family would band together to find Chickadee. Fishtail would help the women on the trail. Animikiins took some fresh maple sugar, dried fish, his rifle, ammunition, and a blanket roll. Omakayas and Animikiins tried to be brave for each other, but when they said good-bye their eyes swelled with tears.

"I will not rest until I find him," said Animikiins. "I will bring our boy home."

"I will not rest until he is with us again," said Omakayas. She struggled for breath. It felt like a stick was breaking inside her chest.

Chickadee's parents clung to each other fiercely, then Animikiins turned, hiding his face, and strode quickly away.

Two Strike stood before Omakayas. The mighty woman was ready for anything. She had a small sack of flour, her rifle, ammunition, her bow, a quiver of arrows, her skinning knife, her carving knife, her tobacco knife, her whittling knife, and two extra emergency knives she kept hidden in her leggings.

Although as children they had disliked each other, Omakayas and Two Strike had become as close as sisters as they grew older. Two Strike was grateful to Omakayas and Angeline for bringing up Zozie, whom she loved but didn't know how to care for. Omakayas appreciated the fierce energy of Two Strike and believed that she had inherited the magnificent spirit of Old Tallow, the much beloved old woman who had hunted bears with a spear and worn the yellow feather of a flicker in her hat. Two Strike dressed in an unusual fashion too, but that was not the main resemblance. The resemblance was attitude.

Both Two Strike and Old Tallow had no time for fools or for civilization. They preferred to live alone in the woods and had gotten rid of their husbands as quickly as possible. They had no time for work that women usually did, but preferred to hunt. They were hard and bitter on the outside, but when it came to children, their hearts were soft.

"I will hunt down those two men who stole your Chickadee, you can be sure. I will destroy them," said Two Strike. She made a fist. When Two Strike smiled, there was something wild and frightening in her eyes.

Makoons, who stood behind his mother, was glad that Two Strike loved them. He was happy that their family was under her protection. He would have hated to be either Babiche or Batiste and face the wrath of his father, his grandfather, and Two Strike.

"Miigwech, my sister," said Omakayas.

She reached out and put her arms around Two Strike's shoulders. Although Two Strike stood stiff as a tree in her sister's embrace, it was clear that she was touched. She sniffled loudly, then lifted her voice in a ringing war cry that tingled down Makoons's spine. Besides Omakayas, only Zozie dared embrace Two Strike. And once that was done, this woman of tremendous strength loped along, sworn to find Chickadee.

In a state of sorrow and anxiety, the rest of the family

packed up their camp and prepared to follow. If they lost the trail, the priest had persuaded them all to meet in the biggest settlement for hundreds of miles, the place where Omakayas's brother, Quill, lived, a place called Pembina.

EIGHT

BOUYAH

On and on the horses galloped. Sometimes Chickadee woke and heard the horses picking their way along or plodding through what seemed like mushy ground. Sometimes the horses stopped and he could hear them chewing. It was warm and dark in the sack, so he always fell asleep again. The horses were good runners and had the will and spirit of the best of their kind. Babiche and Batiste were hard men, but they were tender where their horses were concerned. So what Chickadee sensed from inside his mail sack was that although the horses galloped hard, they were also rested from time to time and were allowed to graze when they came across melted areas of rich winter grass.

They came through the Pembina Hills and even managed to cross the Red River. It was in that perilous time just before the ice broke. But Chickadee slept through that crossing. He was asleep when the horses stopped. Then, suddenly, he was in the air again, thrown off the saddle. He was still in the sack. Chickadee woke as he was falling and had no way to brace himself. He rolled over and over before hitting the earth. Luckily the snow where he landed was still soft, and Batiste quickly untied the sack and let him out. The light was blinding at first, after the darkness in the sack. Chickadee rubbed his eyes and looked around.

Where were the trees? Where were the hills? And again, where were the trees?

There was nothing to see as far as his eyes could reach. This was the Plains. It was Bwaan-akiing, the place where the Dakota people live. It was the Red River Valley. It was Pembina country. Chickadee had heard about the Plains. Others in his family had been to the Plains. But nothing had prepared Chickadee for the sight of such emptiness.

He whirled around, panicked by the vast sky.

Batiste was ducking into a small log cabin. Babiche was taking the two brown horses toward a shanty built of pole logs and mud. There was a great hay pile next to it,

nibbled all the way around the bottom by rabbits. As they passed the pile, the horses reached out their long necks and swiped a matted clump of hay to chew.

Batiste came out of the cabin.

"The mice have eaten everything again!" he angrily cried.

"Get over here," yelled Babiche to Chickadee. "Now you'll learn to make yourself useful. If you don't," he leered, his big yellow teeth dripping with spit, "we will chop you up and feed you to our horses. They love the meat of little boys."

The two mild brown horses looked over their shoulders, their eyes reproachful. They didn't look like they ate little boys, thought Chickadee, but he hurried over to the makeshift barn anyway.

"What do you want me to do?"

Babiche swung his big fist lazily at Chickadee, and Chickadee ducked.

"Next time you ask that, my fist will connect with your head. You do what a servant does!"

Chickadee saw a long branch with sticks whittled out and pegged to the ends. He went over and grabbed it. He looked at Babiche, who made digging and pitching motions with his arms.

Chickadee began to dig up the horse manure on the dirt floor. It was half frozen, but he managed to move a small pile out the door into a heap behind the barn. While he worked at this, the two brothers bumbled about their cabin yelling about the mice.

"Get in here," Batiste called out at last.

Chickadee ran to the cabin. It was dark inside. There were only three small openings for light, each covered with a piece of oiled paper. It was almost like being in the sack again.

When Chickadee's eyes adjusted to the dark, he saw that there were heaps of furs and blankets on the floor. There was a small round tin barrel set on legs with a pipe running out of it. Next to it there were piles of dried brown circles of frozen stuff. It was the first time Chickadee had ever seen buffalo dung, or buffalo chips.

"Start a fire!" growled Batiste.

The brothers stomped out, arguing about which of them would take the first shift to deliver the mail. The mail rider would arrive from St. Paul, said Batiste, and he had ridden first last time.

"But I rode last," said Babiche. "So that means . . . I rode last."

"Which means you should go first," said Batiste.

"No, it means I am still tired out," said Babiche.

"Let's send the servant," said Batiste.

"You are funny, my brother," Babiche laughed. "He would get lost in no time. Our ignorant servant doesn't know where to go!"

"He doesn't know how to make a fire, either," said Batiste in a sudden rage. "He is useless! I will hit him over the head and be done with it!"

"Wait," said Babiche. "Look."

Chickadee had moistened a small chip of the buffalo dung with kerosene from the bottom of the brothers' lamp. He'd seen a lamp like this before in a trading store, and knew the oil worked like fat. He began with the small chip and blew the ember carefully to life, then added bit after bit. The dung smoked, but burned quite well when the fire got hot.

"Maybe he is of some use yet," said Batiste. "Let's get our tasty meat and flour, my brother. Let's have our servant make us some bouyah!"

Suddenly, Batiste broke out in song.

Bouyah, bouyah,
It makes a Michif strong!
Straight to the brain,
He never has to strain!

Fills up his belly,
Makes him sweet as jelly!
Makes his hair grow thick!
Makes his mind so quick!
Bouyah!

Babiche laughed so hard his face swelled red.

"Oh, you are *too* funny, my brother!" he choked.

Doubled over, he could barely point out the flour tin and the chunks of old dried-out questionable meat that Chickadee would use in making the trapper's stew. Although he'd never heard the word *bouyah*, Chickadee knew from looking at the bottom of the kettle on the stove just what the brothers expected of him. The old stuff was stuck to the bottom, and covered with mouse droppings. Even the mice had failed to eat it. Batiste told him to add the new stuff on top of the old stuff and boil it all together with melted snow.

Chickadee tried to scrape out the mice droppings, but Batiste grinned and said, "Leave 'em in there, servant. We don't have pepper to season it with!"

So Chickadee filled the kettle with snow. When the snow melted, he boiled some of the old moose and squirrel meat, and he wrapped up what other meat the brothers had managed to save from the mice. He stirred in the flour and boiled it all some more. At the end, Batiste dropped in a whole dead mouse he'd found. Chickadee just kept the bouyah kettle boiling. At last, Batiste took a spoonful and declared the stew was finished.

There were two bowls and two spoons. The brothers divided up the bouyah into the bowls, used the spoons, and left Chickadee to scrape the leavings from the pot with a stick. As he sat on the icy dirt floor of the miserable cabin, eating the awful stuff that kept life in the sons of Zhigaag, several thoughts came to Chickadee.

Bezhig (one), the mice tails weren't so bad, but the feet were hard to chew.

Niizh (two), he would do exactly as the brothers said.

Niswi (three), he would pretend that he enjoyed being their servant. That way, they would let down their guard so he could escape.

Niiwin (four), he would figure out where to escape to. Outside, everything looked the same. Miles and miles of empty, snowy, plains. There were no landmarks. Nothing but the same horizon all around. Snow would quickly fill in the tracks they had left. He would have to be clever.

Naanan (five), he would take care to avoid their fists and feet. And he would not think of Makoons, of Zozie, of his mother or father, until all was dark and the bouyah-stuffed brothers could not see his tears.

Night came soon enough. Although the brothers argued about whether a servant was allowed to sleep near the masters or out with the horses, they ended up giving him one blanket and allowing him to curl up beside the stove so that he could be all the quicker to make their breakfast.

"You will rise at dawn," said Batiste, "while we are still enjoying our sleeps. You will make our breakfast bouyah."

"How shall I make that?" asked Chickadee.

Babiche raised his fist.

"Same as the dinner bouyah?" asked Chickadee quickly.

"Of course, you scrap of stinking hide," said Babiche.

Batiste began to sing again.

Bouyah, bouyah!
The way to start the day!
If your stew is full of hair,
Just spit it out and swear!
If your stew smells like your feet,
There's more of it to eat!
The worse it gives you gas,
The better you run fast!
White people say it's muck,
But it brings the Michifs luck!
Bouyah!

"You are funny, my brother," Babiche said, weeping with pleasure.

In the dark, curled in his blanket, Chickadee mouthed the words that he realized would be repeated at least twenty times each day. If he ever got back to Makoons, he would never, ever say those words, *You are funny, my brother.* Thinking about Makoons led to nothing but tears and Chickadee could feel them breaking from inside of him even as the huge brothers, falling into their sleep, began a soft snoring that deepened and then widened into an avalanche of noise.

NINE

INTO THE PLAINS

As Omakayas trudged along, following the trail that Deydey, Animikiins, and then Two Strike had made, she realized that if they kept going west they would be leaving the shelter and safety of the woods and hills. They would travel out of the trees and rolling prairie into the broad, flat plains. Animikiins had been there on buffalo hunts, but she never had. It frightened her to think that Chickadee was out there, somewhere, in such unfamiliar territory. Fishtail scouted for the little party. Angeline, Yellow Kettle, and Zozie made sure that the dogs pulled along their packs, and gave Nokomis a ride when her legs tired. Omakayas kept Makoons near her at all times. She could hardly bear to let him out of her sight.

On and on the family walked. Nokomis made her way along slowly with her walking stick, holding Zozie's shoulder. The dogs were fitted with harnesses, and they carried the kettles and extra clothing and rolls of bark for shelter. They also carried the big packs of furs that the family would sell in Pembina. Father Genin had decided to go to Pembina, where he was supposed to meet up with another priest who was starting a school. Father Genin had promised to find Omakayas's brother, the twins' Uncle Quill. He would put out the word that the Zhigaag brothers had stolen Chickadee.

Someone in that big town was sure to know where those brothers lived.

As they walked along, the air got warmer, the sky darker, the clouds lower, and bits of snow began to swirl dizzily around them.

"There is a spring snowstorm coming," said Nokomis. "I can feel it all through my bones."

"Let's make camp," said Omakayas. Although a spring blizzard would melt away quickly, it would be dangerous while it lasted. Sometimes, on the Plains, these fast-moving snowstorms even occurred in the beginning of summer. Omakayas had heard about their force, and now she was to experience it.

The trees had grown scarce, and the hills were only mild bumps. They picked the best shelter they could find and set up the birchbark house. Zozie and Omakayas worked quickly and made the bark secure with straps of twine. They heaped snow against the sides for insulation. Nokomis went inside to start the fire.

The snow stopped for a moment, and then the storm hit with a huge blast of wind. The cruel gust took the entire house into the air. Off it went, sailing into the snowy nothingness, tumbling over the icy ground, bouncing off the hard drifts with nothing to stop it.

This was the last time the family would ever make a house of birchbark. Their house blew away, and they never saw it again. Such houses were for the woods. They were now people of the Great Plains. But they hadn't learned yet how to live there.

And there was Nokomis, striker in her hand, nursing a tiny circle of flame that immediately went out.

"Get into the fur packs!" shouted Omakayas.

Each pack of furs was bundled tightly with sinew, but by pulling out the middle furs each one of them could wiggle in. Nokomis and Makoons got in first. The snow began to drive against them, but Omakayas and Zozie tied the packs together before they got in themselves. The dogs curled near, hiding their noses in the warm curls of their tails. All together, in a heap, the family waited out the storm.

Ahead of them, on the banks of the Red River where the snow was deep, Two Strike and Animikiins had caught up with Mikwam. Together, the three made a snow cave and curled up in their blankets to sleep there.

TEN

TWO STRIKE'S KNIVES

The snow had lightly dusted the cabin of Babiche and Batiste before gathering force and moving eastward to bury Chickadee's family. Exhausted from his second day as a servant, his stomach aching from another day of bouyah, Chickadee fell asleep. He slept so hard that he didn't hear the mail carrier arrive from St. Paul.

The man, Orph Carter, had ridden through the storm, knowing that to stop was death. His horse had gone this route before and was now munching from a pile of dried slough grass in the shanty with the two brown horses. Orph crawled into the cabin with the mail sacks and unrolled his blanket. Soon his snores joined forces with the roaring rapids of snores from the brothers. All that sleep noise became a mighty cataract. Chickadee slept right through it.

At first light, while the men were still sleeping, Chickadee crept out of his covers and noticed that there was another lump of blankets in the cabin. He kindled the fire from the banked ashes, and added buffalo chips. Because there was another lump on the floor, which he assumed was a person, Chickadee added an extra big chunk of moldy old meat to the kettle, and slipped out for an extra dollop of snow. As the bouyah slowly warmed, he stirred in the flour. There were also plenty of mice droppings from the night before. No matter how tightly Chickadee put the lid on the kettle, mice somehow got into the stew pot. He was already used to the musty taste.

As the stew heated up, the cabin air filled with the unsavory steam so beloved by the Zhigaag brothers.

"Ah," said Babiche, stirring and yawning, "how good it is to have a servant!"

"Awee," said Batiste, "he creates a good bouyah, this boy. He makes bouyah like our mother used to make!"

The brothers paused and made the sign of the cross and kissed their lips.

"Mon dieu!" they cried. "This boy was well worth stealing."

"Stealing?" Orph Carter had awakened. "You stole him?"

"Har, har, har," said Babiche. "We stole this boy from

the family of Mikwam, Ice, and the hunter Animikiins, whose wife is Omakayas and whose brother is Quill. She has a sister, Angeline, whose husband is Fishtail. They have a grandmother with them and they sometimes travel with a strange woman called Two Strike."

"Two Strike?"

Orph Carter jumped out of his blankets.

"Have some bouyah," said Batiste, spooning a glop of the stuff onto a slab of wood and passing it to Orph.

"Are you fellows crazy?"

"You would be the crazy one," said Babiche, "if you passed up this delicious stew."

Orph pushed away the plank.

"I'd rather eat boiled mice," he said.

"All right," said Batiste, bending over the stew pot, "I'll dig around and get some for you."

"Two Strike? You have stolen some boy from Two Strike? She'll gut you like a fish when she finds out."

"Har?" said Babiche.

"She will lay in wait for you with two knives between her teeth, two knives in her hands, a knife in her hat, knives in her socks. For all I know, that woman carries a knife in her britches too. Those knives will flash out and cut you to ribbons before you can say—"

"More bouyah," said Batiste. "What are you two talking about?"

"A savage and frightening woman," said Babiche, but he

was not worried. "She sounds like just the woman for us, my brother! Har!"

"I'm getting out of here," said Orph. "Take the mail sack. I'm going out to saddle up Sylvia. Poor Sylvia. I'd hoped to get her more rest. But I don't want to be here when Two Strike comes after this boy."

Babiche and Batiste spooned their stew hastily into their mouths, tossed down the bowls and spoons to be licked clean by mice, and picked up the sacks of mail.

"We'll ride out too," said Babiche, "not because we are afraid of this Two Strike, but because we have taken a blood oath pledge to deliver this precious mail."

As he bolted out the door, Orph pointed at Chickadee.

"And what about him?"

"We'll pop him in a mail sack and take him along," said Batiste.

"Oh, no," groaned Chickadee. "Not the mail sack again."

Batiste raised his fist.

Orph Carter cried out: *"Do. Not. Strike. Him."*

Orph leaped onto his horse, and shouted as he wheeled to gallop south. "Don't you fellows know why she's got the name Two Strike?"

Orph kept yelling the reason, and they might have learned it, too, but as he galloped away in delirious haste, his voice was cut off by wind.

"I'll climb into the mail sack myself," said Chickadee, bolder now that he knew the brothers would not punch him. "It would be better if you left me here, though. That way, when Two Strike tracks me  down. There will just be me. I promise I will tell her that you treated me well!"

The two brothers looked at each other. Then Babiche shrugged. Batiste shuffled his feet around in the snow.

"We would actually *like* to meet this ferocious female," said Batiste, "and the fact is . . . you tell him, Babiche."

"The fact is," said Babiche with a deep, heartfelt sigh, "although it has been a short time, our affections, they grow quick! We have actually begun to *like* you. Once we *like* a person we can never part with him! Har! Har! Awee!"

"We feel this way about few things," said Batiste, stuffing Chickadee gently down into the mail sack. "Liking leads to love. Our horses, Brownie and Brownie, we love them with all the passion in our souls. And each other of course, we love. We do *not* like our father, but we will forever love our mother, the miraculous saint!"

"The saint!"

The last sight Chickadee saw that day was the brothers making the cross over their chests, and kissing their fingers, just the way they did the first time they mentioned their mother.

Maybe it is sign language for mother, thought Chickadee. But the black robe priest made that sign too. Of course, priests have mothers. . . . I wonder if their mothers wear black robes too. . . .

With the mail sack shut, the darkness, and Babiche's woolly vest cradling him again, Chickadee became drowsy.

The horses had stopped. Chickadee was gently lowered to the ground in the mail sack. Babiche let him out.

"There is trouble, my little servant friend," said Babiche. "Look."

On the winter-grassy ground still littered with bits of snow, lay Batiste. He was moaning incoherently, clutching his stomach.

"I blame myself," said Babiche. "Last night, while you were sleeping, we took out a bottle of rotgut whiskey. Batiste is very sensitive. Now his gut is rotting. Terrible!"

There were tears in Babiche's eyes.

"And just as bad, Brownie and Brownie!"

Chickadee noticed that the two horses were panting strangely, foaming at the mouth, and their heads were hanging low.

"There must have been some jimsonweed in their hay. It makes them loco-crazy. We must go on somehow," said Babiche. "The mail must be delivered! Can you carry this sack?"

Chickadee tried to pick it up, but he couldn't budge it.

"Can you carry Batiste?"

Chickadee tried to pick up Batiste, but he couldn't even manage to hold up one of his heavy tree legs.

"Can you lead the horses?"

Chickadee took the reins.

Babiche looked wildly from his brother, to the heavy mail sack, and back to his brother again. He groaned as if he lay beneath a terrible weight.

"Which to choose? Do I carry my brother? Do I carry the mail? Even with my vast strength, I cannot carry both!"

The horses seemed drunk, rolled their eyes, neighed sadly and softly, spat up green saliva.

"Please tell me what to do, little servant friend," said Babiche. "Do I carry the mail, which my blood oath compels me to deliver, or do I carry my brother, whom I love beyond all things except my sainted mother, the horses, and now, perhaps you?"

Babiche crossed his chest and kissed his fingers with tragic desperation.

"What would you do?" Babiche asked, his eyes filling with tears.

"I would carry my brother first, then lay him down and go back for the mail. Then repeat. Over and over until you get there. Meanwhile, I would send my servant back to the barn with the sick horses."

"Not only are you a master cook," said Babiche, "but you are wise. We will follow your plan."

So Babiche hoisted his heavy brother onto his back and staggered forward, leaving the mail in its sack on the ground. Chickadee tugged the reins and the addled horses followed him.

"Au revoir!" called Babiche.

"Gigawaabamin!" cried Chickadee.

They began to walk in opposite directions.

ELEVEN

RIVER BREAK

Omakayas woke in silence and poked her head out of the pack of furs. The wind and snow had stopped. It was near dawn, the stars were out, and the air was warm. Omakayas took a pinch of tobacco from the pouch at her waist and put it on the ground.

"Miigwech," she said to the Southern Thunderbirds. A southern wind had blown the snow away. There was the scent of spring in the air. The family huddled together, relieved. In her heart, Omakayas said a desperate prayer, begging the Creator to keep Chickadee safe.

From a low bush nearby, she heard the soft call of a chickadee, and she smiled in hope. Omakayas and Nokomis built a fire to boil some tea and warm their stomachs. They ate some dried meat flavored with maple sugar. Before dawn, they hitched up their dogs and started walking. They went toward the Red River, for when they reached it they would follow it north, toward Pembina. But in the blizzard, they had lost the trail.

Mikwam, Two Strike, and Animikiins woke in their cave of snow to the noise of dripping water. They had hollowed out their snow cave in the roots of a great tree on the banks of the Red River. It was a cave that led farther back into the earth, but the back wall was a heavy mat of dirt, leaves, and sticks.

As the three of them oriented themselves to the light, there was suddenly a great cracking crash behind them. With a gust of odorous steam, a huge bear scrambled and squeezed by them. The bear liberated itself so suddenly from its den, and was so surprised by its visitors, that in a moment it was gone and the three humans were blinking their eyes and rearranging themselves. Two Strike was out the entrance in a flash, but instead of following the bear, she stood rooted to the riverbank.

Before them, they could see the ice was starting to break up. From their den deep in snow, earth, and roots, they hadn't realized the ice had already begun to jam and melt. Already, the river was too dangerous to cross.

There was no trail for them to follow. They would have

to meet the others in Pembina.

"Nevertheless, we will find that boy," Two Strike said to the river. She hit Animikiins across the shoulders. It was her way of comforting him.

Animikiins climbed to the top of the bank. His face was still. He scanned the horizon to all sides, then he reached into his pouch and put a pinch of tobacco on the ground. He prayed to the spirits, the aadizookaanag.

"Please help us find Chickadee."

TWELVE

THE STRANGE FAMILY

Chickadee made his way along the tips of melting snowdrifts and the edges of mush sloughs. As he walked along, he argued with himself.

"Am I the servant of Babiche and Batiste, or am I their little friend? Babiche gave me the horses to bring safely back to their barn. However, I was stolen. I am lonesome. I want to go home."

Chickadee turned around and asked Brownie and Brownie.

"Must I be loyal to the brothers who stole me?"

The horses pawed the ground and drooled. They gave Chickadee unfocused, dreamy stares, then bent their heads down and ate some winter grass sticking up out of the snow. Chickadee let them eat. The grass was probably good medicine for them.

"No," decided Chickadee.

He tugged the horses along, and as he walked he spoke aloud.

"My mother cries for me, my brother is lonely for me, my sister Zozie sighs. My father holds my mother's hands in his and prays for my return. My Nokomis wipes her old eyes."

Imagining all of the grief his family felt put him in a desperate mood, and tears of frustration filled his eyes. He stopped in the trackless, featureless, sky-filled, and windy world.

"I must go to them," he said. "The only way I know to get to them is find the river, and then follow it north."

Once he had made a decision, Chickadee felt better. He began to trudge along in the direction of the river. The horses, sensing that he had a destination in mind, seemed to regain their senses. They followed with an eager gait and stopped spitting foam. Chickadee didn't have to coax them along. They walked for several hours. Chickadee got hungry, then hungrier, and at last so hungry that he longed for the bottom of that pot of bouyah. He imagined the stick he'd used to scrape the crud on the bottom into his mouth.

"If only there were something to *eat*," he said to the

horses. But there wasn't anything to eat. Just streaks of old snow and winter grass sticking up in tufts or crushed down in soft packs. A rabbit might be good, but he had no jack-pine root or any sort of twine to snare one. When he got to the river, perhaps he could catch a fish—if he could make a fish trap. There was a small flint and striker in the pouch at his waist.

The river seemed his best bet. But would he ever reach it? Or would he starve first, he wondered.

Suddenly, there it was. But it wasn't the frozen bridge it had been when the brothers had crossed in the night. It was swollen, gray, swift, and lethally cold. The ice had gone out, shattering trees in its violent passage, and making the river impassable all along its route.

For a long time, Chickadee stood with the horses. He watched the roiling gray water as it churned frozen slabs of ice along in its rapid flow. They lowered their heads and munched grass. Chickadee put a few pieces of grass in his mouth, just for the taste.

Discouraged, Chickadee walked along the banks, then away from the river. It was rising so fast he was afraid that he and the Brownies could be swept in. As he walked, Chickadee moved slower and slower. He was weak and tired. He turned to Brownie and Brownie.

"You're going to have to give me a ride. First you, Brownie, then you, Brownie. One after the next. I am too weak to keep on walking."

With his last bit of strength, Chickadee climbed on top of one of the Brownies. He tied the reins of the other Brownie to his saddle, then leaned forward, tangled his fists in the horse's mane, and lay his head down on its neck.

Chickadee didn't sleep, he was just very weak. He tried to steer Brownie toward the river, but of course when a horse is left to its own devices it will go back to the safety of its barn. So late that day, in spite of his decision to escape the brothers, Chickadee found himself back at their cabin.

"Oh, yai!"

He was disappointed, but he slipped off Brownie and took off both horses' saddles. The brothers had roughly fenced in an area beside the shanty of a barn. There was

enough old grass in for the horses to browse. The horses nickered and snorted. They pawed up clumps of grass from the snow. They seemed happy enough.

"Now for me," said Chickadee. "Let's see what the mice have left."

He went into the stinking cabin and began to rummage around among the tins and sacks where the brothers kept their food. Everything was gone, it seemed, cleaned right out. There was only a bit of flour in the bottom of a sack. Even the mice were gone. They were finding more food outside of the cabin, now, than inside. Chickadee continued looking. Finally, at the bottom of a metal box, he found two things—a striker and fire-steel, which might come in handy so he put them in the pouch that hung from his belt. He found a ball of twine, handy also, and a tiny ball of pemmican—a mixture of pounded meat, berries, and fat. Food! He shouted with joy. It was surely old and slightly rancid, but he went outside and ate it, leaning against the pole walls in the fading sun. He listened to the wind boom around him, and drank from a bowl of melted snow.

He ate slowly, appreciating every stale nibble. It wasn't much. But his stomach stopped aching and his body grew warm in the sunshine, and comfortable. To the north, a small speck appeared on the horizon. He watched as it enlarged, wavering, and slowly came into focus.

The thing was a wagon drawn by an ox. There was a

driver up front, dressed in black robes, a priest. In back there were a number of huge gray creatures that resembled birds. Chickadee had heard that the white people had some animals the Anishinabeg had never seen before. He had seen a pig, a gookoosh. He had never seen the baka'akwen, the chicken. He had heard that they had an animal with a long gray snout with feet like boulders and enormous ear flaps. He had heard of the long-necked one, spotted, that could see over the tops of trees. His grandfather had once been to a city, and had seen these animals in iron houses like big traps.

Could this be one of these new animals?

Chickadee moved cautiously around the side of the house, and decided not to give himself away. The only place he could find to hide was the stack of slough grass. So he climbed to the top and lifted up a heavy mat of hay and slipped underneath. He had placed himself exactly where he could see all that went on when the wagon pulled into the yard.

Peeping out from under the hay, Chickadee saw immediately that he had been wrong about the creature. The gray wings were pieces of cloth, long stiff veils. They surrounded the faces of six white women, who also wore long cloaks of gray. Their hands were encased in gray mittens, and their feet were dainty in black lace-up boots. When the wagon stopped, they hopped down from the back. There was a small black dog with them, a serious-looking dog who jumped down to scout the area as if to make sure it was safe. At once, he barked at Brownie and Brownie, and trotted back and forth between the women and the horses as if to make sure they knew there was danger near.

Chattering like squirrels, the women in strange gray dresses went to investigate the cabin. Each ventured in and came out quickly, waving the air away from her nose.

The black robe, who wore a flat black hat and had a rosy face and twinkling blue eyes, laughed.

"We'd best be on our way," he said. "Come along, Sisters."

So, thought Chickadee, these were the black robe's six sisters. This was a family—an odd family who dressed much differently than most, but probably harmless. Still, he decided to remain hidden. And if not for the little black dog, he probably would have gone unnoticed.

The black dog started barking. Worse, it threw itself against the haystack. Chickadee could feel the vibrations every time it smacked into the hay below. The little dog was determined to tell its family that there was someone in the haystack. Some animal, they thought.

"Gertrude probably smells a rat," said one of the Sisters. "Come, Gertrude. Here, Gertrude!"

But the dog barked even more urgently, threw itself madly, insistently, until it caused the hay to tremble and slide. Chickadee had to adjust his weight.

"I saw something move," said the priest. "If it was a rat, it was enormous."

"Come, Gertrude!"

The Sisters called the dog to them in alarm. They did not want to see an enormous rat and wanted to leave the stinking cabin and the haystack well behind them. All of the Sisters, that is, except the youngest and most curious one.

She was small, and a brown curl the same color as the Brownies coat peeked under the gray contraption on her head.

"I'll get Gertrude, and find out what she's so excited about. I'm not afraid of a rat, no matter how big!"

"Sister Seraphica! Please!"

But Seraphica picked her way through the muddy snow and straw of the Zhigaag brothers' yard until she reached the dog.

"Gertrude, what is it?" she said in her gentle voice.

The dog went wild, hopping high and smashing its little body against the hay.

Seraphica laughed and stood on tiptoe. She peered up into the stack of grass and looked straight into Chickadee's eyes.

"It's not a rat," she called. "It's a . . . boy, I think!"

The priest came running.

"Look, Father," she pointed.

Chickadee tried to sink into the hay, but he had hunkered down as far as he could.

"I can't see anything," said the priest.

"If it is a boy, then he's hungry," said Seraphica. Her face was round and sweet. She had green eyes with long black eyelashes, and a small round nose. Her mouth was generous and her smile was wide and full.

She rummaged in a bag tied to her waist and took out a piece of bread. She held the bread out in the tips of her fingers. It was fragrant, fresh, and before Chickadee could stop himself, his hand darted out from beneath the grass and snatched the roll from her hand.

"There," said Seraphica. "See?"

The other Sisters leaned over the edge of the wagon. Even from there, they could hear the munching and smacking of Chickadee enjoying the bread. He spat out a strand of grass. The priest smiled.

"Let's try to coax him out."

The priest and the Sisters hadn't much to eat themselves, but each contributed a morsel. Seraphica held each bit out, an offering. And every time Chickadee smelled what she held, he reached out and grabbed it. He meant to stay hidden, but his hunger was just too much for him.

"Will you come out now?" asked Seraphica. She held out her open hand. Chickadee tried to burrow farther down, but he knew it was no use.

"Come on, we won't hurt you," she said. Of course, as she spoke English, Chickadee could not understand all of what she said. But the tone of her voice was so smooth and sweet he knew that she meant no harm. He peeped his head out.

"Ah!" cried the Sisters.

"He's a terrible mess," said Seraphica. "Neglected, so sad."

"Can we take him with us?"

"Yes, yes, let's!"

"He is such a nice-looking boy under all that dirt!"

The priest put his hands out, too.

"Come along," he said. "We have a place prepared for you!"

"You'll be fed, warm, happy!"

The Sisters called melodiously and the priest was so pink and jolly that Chickadee found himself sliding from the slough grass into their arms. Seraphica brought him to the wagon, and the Sisters laughed and held their noses, but climbed in and made a place for him in the straw with the little black dog. The dog had the sort of mouth that curls up in a cheerful smile. He seemed to grin as Chickadee settled in beside him. How could a boy resist what seemed to be a happy family? From the few words he understood, they called the priest Father and there was a woman in the wagon, worn and stern, whom they called Mother.

"Mother," said Seraphica, "wasn't it a blessing that we found this boy? He might have starved to death, the poor orphan."

"Orphan, my foot," said Mother. "He is a filthy savage."

"Mother, you shouldn't say that," said the jolly priest.

"Don't you dare tell me what to say," said Mother. "He could kill us in our sleep."

"He's a little boy!" said Seraphica.

"Just you keep on eye on him," said Mother. She fixed a cold gray eye on Chickadee and held him in her glare.

As Chickadee bounced along on the straw bedding with the dog, the six Sisters, the Mother and the Father, he didn't know if he was leaving his family behind or if, through this new adventure, he might be brought closer to them. He knew only that to stay behind was impossible. He would certainly have starved before the two brothers returned. And once they did return, he would once again have been their servant.

Wherever he ended up, he hoped he'd find an Anishinabe who could bring word back to his parents. As the wagon went on and on, roughly following the path of the river, he tried talking to the nice Sister, the one who pointed to herself and said Seraphica.

Chickadee pointed to himself, and said the word for Chickadee in Ojibwe, which is Gijigijigaaneshiinh. No matter how hard Seraphica tried, her tongue got tangled up when she repeated the word. But once, when the wagon stopped and the Sisters got out to eat their tiny scraps of food and to pray, a small bird landed in the bushes near the wagon. Chickadee looked at the bird for a long time, and it looked back at him.

"Stay with me," he said to his namesake. The bird seemed to understand.

Chickadee took Seraphica's sleeve and pointed to himself, to the bird, and back again. She understood.

"Your name means Chickadee!"

Excited, she told the other women, who smiled at him and told Seraphica that the name was perfect for such a thin and lively little boy.

Only the one called Mother frowned and gave Seraphica a sour look.

"He'll be baptized and given a proper name," she said, "a saint's name. How typically pagan, to be named after a bird!"

For two days the little wagonload of women traveled. At night they all slept, curled in the straw. During the day, Chickadee saw them secretly wincing whenever the wagon jounced over a big rock. He had the soft straw to sit on, while they were arranged across two hard board benches. At last, they reached a river crossing.

At this crossing, there was a ferryboat that ran along underneath a huge cable. The river was much calmer here—though still icy and gray and flowing fast. It would be possible to cross.

The priest and the ferry owner coaxed the ox aboard and secured the wagon. Then the Sisters stood in a bunch and held tight to the sides of the barge. Seraphica held on to Chickadee and the dog crouched near his feet. If the ferry were to sway out into the river, if the cables were to snap, they would swing out into the treacherous current for a wild and deadly ride. The Sisters prayed fervently, with their eyes closed, all except for Seraphica. Her eyes were open, and her lips moved. It looked to Chickadee like she was enjoying the ride.

When at last the party was on the other side of the river,

Chickadee's first thought was that now he could escape and follow the river north. It would lead him back home, eventually, although he was farther away than he'd ever been. For a while, the wagon followed the river north. Then suddenly a rutted trail appeared and it veered east. Chickadee watched each small landmark carefully. He was elated to again see trees, then sloughs, then rolling hills and land that looked like home, even though much of it was torn up. Now he saw small board houses painted white or even red. He'd only seen a trader's house painted this way before. Fluffy white and rust-colored birds ran around these houses. From his mother's description, he knew that these were chickens. They'd entered farm country, settled by tall people with pale eyes and sun-bright hair. At last, after the endless journey, the wagon stopped outside a log cabin with a cross fixed over the door.

There were two other log cabins beside the first one, and a barn behind. One of the smaller cabins belonged to all of the Sisters and the Mother. The Father had the other cabin, which was divided into a small room for him and a larger room with several small tables in it.

In the front of the room there was a smooth piece of wood as black as river rock. Father took a white stick in his hand and traced marks on the blackness. Then, with his other hand, he erased them and made other marks.

"Chalkboard," said Father.

He gave the white stick to Chickadee. He imitated the

marks that Father had made, and Father laughed.

"I believe you'll have no trouble learning the alphabet," he said. "This is a school. Can you say school?"

Chickadee looked at him quizzically.

"Oh well, it doesn't matter. You'll learn soon enough. For now, you can sleep here, in the corner."

He showed Chickadee a tiny area where several blankets were piled.

"The other students will come in a few days," said Father, patting Chickadee's head. He tugged one of Chickadee's braids and said, "Don't worry. Mother Anthony will cut these off for you."

Chickadee had no idea what the priest had just said, but before he went to sleep, he looked all around the room. On the desk, in an open box, he saw a small knife. Chickadee had been taught never, ever, to steal. But he broke this rule. Something about the strange family made him uneasy. He did not trust the Mother. He took the knife.

THIRTEEN

A DESPERATE MATTER

The next morning, Chickadee woke to a rhythmical brushing noise. He peeped out of his blanket to see Sister Seraphica on her hands and knees, scrubbing the wooden floor. As she scrubbed, she began to hum a lovely tune and Chickadee crept from his blankets to listen.

Seraphica stopped, sat back on her heels, and laughed.

"Come here, little fellow," she said. She gestured in such a friendly way that Chickadee stood up and walked over to her. She took a piece of bread from her pocket.

"I saved this for you," she said.

Chickadee still did not understand a word anybody said, but when Seraphica spoke to him she also made gestures with her hands.

"Mother Anthony has begged some clothes for you," she said. "Today she means to clean you up. She isn't the gentlest person, but she only wants to help you. Oh, here she comes!"

The unsmiling Mother stamped into the room, right over Seraphica's clean floor. She held a pair of overalls, a mended shirt, and leather tie-up shoes.

"Bring in the washtub," she told Seraphica. "I've got the water heated up. I'll use your scrub brush."

"Oh, Mother, no! It's much too rough!"

"He's got the dirt of the ancients on him, caked in," said Mother. "I'll use some of my strong lye soap."

"That stings!" Seraphica made a face. "Oh, you poor boy!"

Chickadee saw her look of concern, and warily stepped backward. Mother Anthony shook the clothes at him.

"These weren't easy to get! You'd better appreciate them!"

Chickadee was wearing a pair of soft skin trousers, a buckskin shirt with fringe down the sides, which his mother had decorated with porcupine quills. His moccasins were lined with fur and kept his feet warm, while the leggings he wore doubled the insulation of his trousers. He had on a warm woolen vest and, in addition, he usually wore a pair of fur mitts and a fur-lined hood. But when Babiche had stolen him, he'd been sleeping without his hood and mitts.

It was lucky that the night had been cold and he'd kept on his vest and moccasins. From the way Mother gestured, Chickadee began to understand that she expected him to exchange his warm clothes for these poor rags.

He stepped back farther, until he was standing against the wall. Seraphica carried a large wooden tub into the room. Another of the Sisters brought a bucket of water. She poured it into the tub. Mother left and came back with a blanket and a steaming kettle and a strange smelling waxy yellow cake. She poured the steaming kettle of water into the tub and then pointed at the tub, at Chickadee, the tub, Chickadee. He edged along the side of the room, toward the door. But Seraphica was there, smiling.

"Now, don't be scared," she said. "It won't last forever. And you'll feel so good and clean when it is done."

Seraphica took his hand and drew him over to the tub. She tugged off his vest and then began to take off his shirt. Chickadee struggled out of her grip, but Mother was there and the other Sister, too.

"Help!" cried Mother.

Holding on to Chickadee, she and the others unlaced his moccasins, his leggings, removed his shirt, his pants. They rolled everything into a ball, and then plunged him straight into the hot water.

Although at that moment Chickadee was covered with ground-in dirt, it was because he'd been living with Babiche and Batiste. Omakayas kept her boys very clean, and their clothing as well. They bathed in cold water every single day, even in the winter, when they used half-melted snow. Being dunked in steaming hot water was a shock, and Chickadee yelled out in fear. But Mother had the scrub brush out and was sawing it across his back, leaving painful welts into which she rubbed the harsh lye soap. Now Chickadee cried out in pain.

Sister Seraphica tugged at Mother Anthony's wrists.

"Oh, Mother Anthony, please! You're hurting him!"

"Don't be disrespectful, girl!" cried Mother Anthony.

Chickadee struggled, twisting and kicking to get away. But before Chickadee could wiggle away, Mother Anthony snatched up a pair of scissors to cut off his braids. When Chickadee saw the sharp scissors in her hands, he was sure that he was going to die.

With a desperate lunge, he ripped himself from the Sisters' grip and popped out of the tub. He grabbed his ball of clothes. Then, with a tremendous leap, he cleared the table and raced out the door. He didn't stop once he got outside, but kept on running across the muddy yard and on into the safety of the woods. And even then, as the brush closed over behind him, he kept on running. With the ball of clothing under his arm, he sped as fast as he could through the underbrush, in which direction he couldn't tell. It didn't matter. He heard their calls at first, and then their calls died out and there were only the sweet sounds of the woods.

After some time, he entered a great stand of pine and all he heard was the sound of wind tossing high in the pine needles. That sound had always lulled him to sleep. He felt better, but still he kept going. When he'd run until he was exhausted, he stopped and put on his old, familiar clothing. He tied on his leggings and his moccasins. He looked around carefully, for any sign they were following. He listened. His heart thumped wildly, but there was no sound of pursuit.

Chickadee breathed more easily, took stock of where he was. Moss clung to the colder, moister sides of the huge pine trees, telling him which way to go. So he started walking the way the trees pointed. North. Giiwedin. Home.

FOURTEEN

SETTING UP HOME

As Chickadee set off for home, his family met in Pembina, at the cabin of Chickadee's uncle, Quill. It wasn't a very large cabin, and everyone was crowded into it talking.

"Quill isn't here," said his wife, Margaret.

The grown-ups sat wrapped in their blankets on the pounded earth floor and ate the dried moose meat that Omakayas had brought along, seasoned with the new maple sugar.

"Where has he gone?" asked Omakayas.

"Quill was hired on the oxcart train down to St. Paul,"

said his wife proudly. "He made his own cart and is hauling for the fur trader."

"Our little brother has become a responsible man!" laughed Angeline, nodding at Omakayas.

The packs of furs that Animikiins, Two Strike, Fishtail, and Mikwam had worked hard for all winter were stacked around them. Two Strike had also killed a beaver on the way to Pembina, and its skin was stretched out on a willow hoop. The beaver meat was boiling on the little stove that heated the house.

Quill had surprised everyone. From a wild boy who drove his sister Omakayas half crazy, he'd become a young man. He was not a completely sensible young man, but he'd managed to build a cabin and even plant some potatoes. This was all because he wanted to keep his wife, who threatened to leave him if he kept up his old, wild ways.

Margaret was half French and half Ojibwe—both sides of her were no-nonsense sides, Makoons thought. This was the first time the family had met her, and Makoons could tell that although she tried to be nice, her real feelings showed through.

"Come in," she had said. But her face said, *Stay out.* "Sit down and have some tea," she had said out loud, but her face said, *I wish you'd go away.*

The inside walls were whitewashed, pasted over with written papers. A bed, covered with thick blankets, was pushed against one wall, and there were two chairs at a small wooden table. Deydey sat on one chair. Margaret gave the other to Nokomis. Everyone stood uncomfortably until Margaret asked them to sit down on the bed. A tiny woodstove with a pipe sticking into the wall glowed hotly. Margaret put more wood into the fire, and set a kettle of water on top to boil. Everyone ran out of things to say, suddenly, and stared at the floor. Margaret was silent until Deydey began to speak to her in her language, Metis, which was a combination of French and Ojibwe, just like her family. Deydey had learned the language when he was a little boy. Margaret smiled a little, and then Deydey made her laugh. She got up, moved a large pot onto the stove, and, still talking to Deydey, warmed up some stew and made a bannock.

As everyone ate, Deydey explained everything that Margaret had told him in her language. Margaret had described how she had persuaded Quill to settle down, make a garden, and pray. She described the long expeditions to hunt buffalo that the two went on together, with her family. Deydey said that Margaret was very strict about going to the Catholic church, and that once she found out why the family had left the sugar bush, she had said she would pray hard for Chickadee's return.

The family began to talk to Margaret through Deydey,

who translated everything they said.

"Since we know who took our Chickadee," said Oma-kayas, "we have agreed to intercept them here when they deliver the mail."

"Even now, we have our lookouts, Two Strike, Fishtail, and Animikiins," said Nokomis. "They will not let those skunks get away."

"We will wait here," said Mikwam, "for Quill to return."

Margaret looked worriedly at her bed. Then her face brightened, and she told Deydey something that took a long time to explain.

Deydey nodded from time to time as she spoke, and then he looked very thoughtful. Finally, he told the family what he had heard.

"Margaret is urging us to stay in Pembina. She says that so many families have moved on to the other town, St. Joseph, because of the flooding, that there are abandoned cabins. She says that Quill misses us and wishes we were here to hunt the buffalo. She misses her own family, who have moved even farther west. She wishes we would stay here, only not in her bed." Deydey smiled as he said the last sentence.

"We are only here to collect Chickadee and sell the winter's furs," said Omakayas. She and Animikiins lived far off in the bush for a good reason—wherever people gathered, so did illness. "We will bring Chickadee back with us," she said.

At the mention of his brother's name, Makoons felt his spirits sink. He leaned against his mother. He felt that only she missed his twin as much as he did.

"Nimama," he whispered, " I dreamed about Chickadee again last night."

Omakayas put her arm around his shoulders. Every bite of the bannock was tasty and soft, especially dipped in the tea and maple syrup that Margaret provided. His grandfather winked at Makoons in sympathy. But still he was so lonely for Chickadee that every bite, every sip, made him lonelier. He couldn't help wondering if his brother had anything as good to eat. He couldn't help wanting to share.

"My brother's wife," said Omakayas at last, through Deydey, to Margaret, "it has been a good visit. We will find somewhere else to sleep tonight. If we have Chickadee, we'll be warm and happy anywhere we camp!"

"Wait," said Yellow Kettle suddenly, "and listen and think. We have come so far. This is our chance to see your brother, Quill, my son. If there is a place for us to live, we can stay and gather up our winter's food. It might be a good idea."

"There is another reason," said Deydey. "There is a school here." He pointed at the wall. "The twins must learn to read, and to write the white man's language. If they do not do this, everything will be stolen from them."

"Not if we go back! Not if we live far from everybody!"

cried Omakayas, holding Makoons.

"There is good in what everyone says," said Nokomis. "But we cannot decide this until we know for sure whether we can stay in one of these left-behind houses."

Everyone agreed that this was true, and in addition, that they would have to wait for Chickadee's return *somewhere*. But not in Margaret's bed, as she was very protective of her pretty bed, it was clear!

As the family took leave of Margaret she entreated them to think over all she had said. This time, when she spoke, her face did not have the opposite expression. She meant it. She had begun to like Quill's family very much and, although she didn't want them to take over her carefully groomed cabin, she wanted them, very much, to stay.

FIFTEEN

AT THE MERCY OF TWO STRIKE

"I will not stir," said Two Strike. She sat on a rock and sharpened each of her knives on another rock. She stared into the distance. So did Animikiins and Fishtail. After a time, the air grew dark and cold. Fishtail made a fire. Animikiins took out some dried pemmican. They ate. They slept. They woke again, and waited. Two Strike kept a lookout while the two men hunted. The air grew dark and cold again, and Fishtail built up the fire. Animikiins roasted the rabbits he'd caught. The three ate, slept, and waited again by the rock.

At first there was just a dot on the horizon. It was a

curious dot. After it appeared, it disappeared. Then after a time it appeared again. The dot seemed to go forward, then backward, to enlarge and shrink. It wavered and sank out of sight. When it finally got big enough so that the watchers could tell it was a man carrying a large load, Two Strike growled.

"Something is wrong here," said Animikiins.

"Let's find out," said Fishtail.

The three ran toward the strange figure and soon reached Babiche, who staggered beneath a tremendous weight. His brother was on his back, groaning and half conscious. The huge canvas mail sack was at his feet.

For all of his other faults, Babiche had two fierce loyalties. He had carried his brother, then the mail sack, then his brother again, whenever he could not walk. Somehow, as the result of this extreme effort, the two brothers and the mail sack had continued along the trail.

"Merci, mon dieu! Merci beaucoup!" cried Babiche. "Come help me my friends . . . and, ah!"

Suddenly he recognized that Two Strike was not a man. Not only that, but she had a knife between her teeth and two knives in her hands and was running straight at him. In a flash the words of Orph Carter rang in Babiche's head and he sank to his knees.

He dumped his brother on the ground and put his beefy hands in the air.

"Pardon! Pardon!" he cried.

In a bound, Two Strike reached him and loomed over him. Animikiins was right behind.

"Where is Chickadee?"

Babiche's eyes welled with tears.

"What do you mean? Chickadee? You want a little bird? I haven't seen one!"

"Gaawiin, you lying son of a skunk," said Two Strike. "We want the boy you stole. Where is he?"

"Boy?" Babiche gave a frozen grin.

On the ground, Batiste had stopped groaning. He was pretending to be dead.

"If you don't answer me right now," said Two Strike, "all the knives come out!"

"Oh yes, now I remember," Babiche blubbered. "The boy wanted to go with us."

Animikiins grabbed Babiche around the throat and lifted him with one hand.

"We took the boy!" Babiche gasped. "Awee! I admit this! But my friend, you have *two*. Both the same! Could you not spare one?"

Animikiins could not help his hand from squeezing. His desperation was the boundless desperation of a father who loves his son. Behind them, Fishtail restrained Two Strike from using at least three of her knives on Babiche right then. Babiche gestured wildly for Animikiins to let go of his neck so he could talk.

Animikiins dropped him, and Babiche choked, rubbing his neck.

"Talk, and be quick about it," said Fishtail.

"When, ah, my brother took sick I sent the boy back to our little house with the horses. He kindly took them. He was a very good serv— Ah, boy! He's probably back there by now with the horses, a cozy fire going, a nice pot of bouyah cooking."

"Wretch! What are you talking about! Servant?" Two Strike said.

"We made him our servant, yes," said Babiche in a tiny voice. "But now, great lady, my brother and I will serve you! We will be happy to serve you!"

"Chickadee should be your master," cried Two Strike.

"And where is this house?" Animikiins was becoming dangerous with frustration. Servant indeed! His little son!

Babiche trembled as he gave directions to the cabin. Even as he shuddered, though, he was filled with admiration for Two Strike. He looked at his brother. Batiste had opened one eye just a crack, and its gleam told Babiche that he thought Two Strike was magnificent.

"We have treated the boy like our own son," cried Babiche. "Because we heard of the beauty of this vision before us. This woman, Two Strike."

Two Strike bent over and snarled at him. This snarl completely melted the heart of Babiche. He begged her to marry him—and his brother, too—right on the spot.

"And the horses will be our wedding gift!" he said.

Two Strike's hand grabbed his throat. "You are lucky to escape with your life," she said. "If I ever see you or your brother again I'll slice you to ribbons, I'll tear you to shreds, I'll grind you to a pulp. I'll destroy you!"

"Oh, what heaven!" cried Babiche. "My heart is already mashed like a boiled potato!"

Batiste lifted his head, dizzy with emotion. He quickly added, "And mine is crushed like a rotten turnip!"

"We are a bouyah of love, boiling for you!" they shouted together.

But the two were calling after a quickly disappearing Two Strike. She and Animikiins had already started running, following along Babiche's trail. Left with the two brothers and the mail sack, Fishtail spoke with furious disgust.

"You can carry your stinking brother," he said. "I will take the mail."

Fishtail soon left Babiche staggering beneath the load of Batiste, and strode into town. He dropped the mail off at the steps of a small wooden church where he saw a priest working. He spoke to the priest for a moment, then continued on until he came to his family. They were just starting out from Quill's cabin.

When Omakayas didn't see either Chickadee or Animikiins, her face fell. She bravely held on to Nokomis, and together the little family listened to Fishtail's story. When he had finished, they sat right down where they were. It was a pretty spot, on a small hill that sloped down to the roiling river. Mikwam and Fishtail took out their pipes, smoked them, prayed, and together the family looked into their hearts. They needed direction. They knew they had to wait here, as patiently as they could. The question was how long.

"We don't know how long," Fishtail said at last. "That is the problem. But I do know that our son is clever, and we have taught him how to live like an Anishinabe."

"Perhaps we think over what Quill's wife told us," said Omakayas slowly. She was reluctant to live in a town but, more than anything, she wanted the return of her son.

"We will not stay with Quill or, rather, not with Margaret," said Yellow Kettle.

Omakayas and Nokomis silently agreed, flashing a look of assurance at each other.

"If there is nowhere to live, we'll make our own cabin," said Mikwam.

"And plant our own garden," said Nokomis. All along the way from the island they came from, far back in the lake, she had gathered seeds from other gardeners. Now she had a pouch of seeds she guarded day and night. She was eager to plant them.

"I have been wanting to live in a cabin like the one we had so long ago," said Mikwam. "When they bring back our Chickadee, we'll have a place ready for us all to live!"

Nokomis smiled at the memory and patted Yellow Kettle's hand. Perhaps some of them were not eager to leave the islands of Lake of the Woods, where the fish were plentiful and the berries grew thick. On the other hand, the only way to find Chickadee was to stay where they were, and to wait.

That very day, the family took their packs of furs to the traders. As they were beautifully prepared and well kept, and as Mikwam and Yellow Kettle were good bargainers, they got the best price possible. Next, the family went to the priest Fishtail had met, Father Belcourt. The first priest, Father Genin, had told Father Belcourt all about the family. Father Belcourt was known to be sympathetic to the Ojibwe and to the Metis. He often came along on the buffalo hunts and provided a blessing, helped the hunters get along, and said a Mass of thanks when the hunt was over.

Now they asked the priest where land was available. Father Belcourt was just leaving the little cabin next to the church, where he lived. He spoke Ojibwe with Mikwam and pointed out a plot of land high enough to stay clear of the river's floodwaters. Many people made the mistake of building too close to the Red River, he said, and it cost them dearly come spring. The land he pointed out had been abandoned. It belonged to a family that had left for

St. Joseph, just as Margaret had said. There was a cabin on it already, the roof collapsed from winter snow. There was even a garden laid out alongside and the beginnings of a pole barn for horses.

"You will need horses out here, on the Plains," said Father Belcourt.

"True enough," said Mikwam.

Omakayas gave Father Belcourt a makak of maple sugar. It was a special basket, with a picture of a wild goose on the side and fit with a clever lid.

"Such nice work," said the priest. "And my favorite food. Nothing beats the excellent taste of your maple sugar!"

His long, grave face brightened with pleasure and he smiled at all of them. As they walked toward the hill, carrying all that belonged to them, his smile became thoughtful. Here was an intelligent and hardworking family. He would like to have them in his church, and the children in his school. He hoped they'd flourish on the side of the hill, and come back to him. He hoped he could save their souls.

That very day, the family set about making themselves a new place to live. Fishtail and Mikwam set the fallen rafters aside and straightened out the log walls. Omakayas and Nokomis mixed mud with broken grass and wood chips to set between the logs. Makoons and Zozie were sent down to the river to haul water. Yellow Kettle fetched wood, chopped it into a pile, and made a fire in a sheltered area where she could cook. The dogs, their harnesses and loads removed, roamed the area and hunted for rabbits.

After hauling bucket after bucket of water, Makoons and Zozie decided to try catching some fish. There were other people by the river catching fish, big fat ones with golden eyes and rough scales. One of them had thrown a smaller fish aside, which Makoons picked up. He whittled two sharp fishhooks from a bit of wood. Each had a coil of strong and slender line from Mikwam, who had bought it along with the other supplies. Zozie sliced the small fish to ribbons, and then she and Makoons baited their hooks.

One fish, another! The fish were biting hard in the spring flood, hungry from their winter's fast. When they had a neat string of fish, they carried them up the hill.

That night Yellow Kettle baked them in the coals of the fire, and seasoned them with maple sugar.

As Makoons ate, he wondered what his brother was eating, and his chest began to hurt all around his heart. He put down his food and crept into his blankets. He put his hand over his face but his tears leaked through his fingers.

SIXTEEN

THE SMALL AND THE FIERCE

Chickadee was alone in the woods. Very alone. He walked as long and as far as he could, then gathered up a pile of leaves for a bed. He still had the fire-steel, flint, and the knife he'd taken from the desk of the priest. Maybe tomorrow night he'd make a fire, but for tonight, he'd not risk it. The smoke might give him away. Hungry, cold, thirsty, and lonely, Chickadee curled into the pile of leaves. As he fell asleep, he too put his hand over his face. Tears leaked through his fingers. He sobbed his brother's name.

The strong spring sun woke Chickadee, and he sat up, scattering leaves all around. He began immediately to walk, and he walked with great purpose, but by the time the sun was high Chickadee was so weak he had to sit down on a rock.

He put his head down on his knees, for he was dizzy with thirst and hunger.

Maybe I will die here, he thought. That thought made him get up and walk again, heading steadily north.

Soon the sun sank deeply through the bare branches of the trees. Chickadee's knees wobbled. His stomach pinched so hard he cried out. He sat down again, his back against a tree. He closed his eyes.

Maybe I will die here, he thought again. And again this thought forced him to rise and travel, although he staggered and reeled along.

The next time his strength gave out, though, Chickadee lay down on the earth. He'd found a patch of sun and it was warm on his face and arms. He did not want to give up, but there was no strength in him. The wish to travel on was there, but his legs were weak as stems of grass. If only he could find water, a bit of food, but water most importantly.

I will die here unless you help me. Please help me, he thought.

He wondered whom he was asking to help him—Gizhe Manidoo, the great, kind spirit? Other helpful spirits, the adizookaanag? Perhaps the memegwesiwag, the little people, spirits of the forest. Or his we'eh, his namesake, perhaps? Who would answer if he spoke aloud?

"Help me, please help me, or I will die here," he said to the air, the trees, and anything else that could hear him.

Immediately, on a thin branch right over his face, a chickadee perched.

This bird spoke to him, not in the voice of a bird, but in a voice he could understand.

"I have been following you, my son," said the chickadee, "and I remember that you insulted me once, but that you were very sorry. You fed me. You asked my pardon. Therefore I will help you now. Do you remember what Nokomis said?"

Chickadee listened and smiled. "I remember," he said. "Nokomis said that small things have great power."

"You remember well!" The chickadee trilled with pleasure. "I do have great power, my little son. And I will help you. Now listen."

The little gray bird with the jaunty black cap told Chickadee that just beyond the trees, and over the next rise, he would find a fresh stream of water. There, too, he would find a rabbit that two hawks had fought over. They had dropped the kill, but in their fury over who should have the rabbit, they had grappled together and held on so tightly that their deathly sharp claws had locked together.

"You will find the rabbit on the ground, and the hawks

close by. The hawks are not my friends, of course. I tease them. But as I am too little to bother with, they try to ignore me. If you help the hawks, and tell them I sent you to their assistance, they will one day return the favor. And now, to give you strength my little son, I will teach you my song."

I am only the Chickadee
Yet small things have great power
I speak the truth.

Chickadee learned the song. It was a short song, as all real Ojibwe songs are. The melody went up and down like the chickadee's song. He sang it over and over with his we'eh, his father and protector.

"Whenever you need my power, you must sing this song. Use it wisely. You can help others with it, too. This song can heal people. Now go on your way!" the bird said.

Then Chickadee stood and his we'eh darted away into the brush, singing the song. Chickadee began to walk just the way he'd been told, following each direction carefully. Whenever he wobbled and felt that he could not go on, he sang the song he'd been given. The song became his own song very quickly. It gave him strength. He could feel the words flow through him and his legs moved with purpose.

At last, walking down a low hill covered with brush,

he found the stream. He raced to its edge, thanked the chickadee, and drank. No water he'd drunk had ever tasted so good.

When Chickadee raised his head and sat back on his heels, he saw the dead rabbit, freshly killed, lying next to him. He stood, strengthened by the water, and looked around. Sure enough—there were the two hawks, their claws clenched, panting in exhaustion. They had been stuck together struggling to get loose for so long that they had no strength left.

"I have come to help you," said Chickadee, approaching them.

The hawks' yellow eyes regarded Chickadee with hatred and cold contempt. He thought he heard their voices, too, though they were as faint as thought.

"We would rather die than have you touch us, human. Anishinabe though you are, we call you death!"

"I will not hurt you," said Chickadee. "I have been given a message."

"A message? From what being?"

The hawks panted and opened their beaks, hissing at him.

"I have a message from the chickadee."

"Ah," said one of the hawks. "That one. He eludes us. He plays tricks on us. We pretend he is too small to bother with. But the truth is we just can't catch him."

"We respect the tiny one," said the other hawk. "He has

different power than ours. No claws. But you see that our claws have got us into trouble."

Chickadee saw that they had locked their claws so fiercely and tightly that they could not spread them out.

"If you do not help us, we will die together," said the hawk. "We are not enemies; in fact, we are sisters. But we were both greedy for the rabbit."

"Which you may have, human," said the other hawk, "as a sign of our gratitude, if you help us."

"Miigwech," said Chickadee, crouching beside the hawks. He carefully unbent each claw, pulling it from the grip of the other hawk. When they were free, they tried to hop apart, but flopped on the earth, powerless.

"We have lost too much strength," gasped one hawk. "Surely, we must die anyway."

"Wait here," said Chickadee.

He ran over to retrieve the rabbit. With his little knife, he skinned away several pieces of the rabbit and fed them to the hawks. He took care not to get his fingers near their razor-sharp beaks. They gulped down the food. Although their yellow eyes were still cold and haughty, there was something friendlier about them once they had eaten.

"You have shared your food with us willingly," said one of the hawks.

"Only our parents share food willingly. We have to fight our way through life. You, although human, we now regard as our child. We are your mothers and must share with you. We have excellent eyesight and we are superb hunters! We will help you wherever you go."

The hawks beat their wings now, feeling the power course through them. The light showed through the lovely scorched red colors of their tails.

"Whenever you find the feather of a hawk, pick it up. It will be a gift for you," said one of the hawks.

Up they flew, beating their powerful wings hard at first, then soaring as they caught the wind.

Chickadee looked down at his feet. There were two red tail feathers, striped with black. Beside the feathers, the rabbit.

Right there, he made camp and kindled a small, hot fire to roast the skinned rabbit. He kept the pelt, too. He could smoke it at his fire overnight and put it inside his moccasins for additional warmth.

As he sat on soft balsam boughs, eating the meat, he hummed the song he'd been taught. He was not so lonely now. He'd been adopted. He had a father, the chickadee, and two mothers who were hawks.

Now that Chickadee had found the stream, his luck improved. If he followed the stream, he'd come to a trail, perhaps, or at least a river. He might find a camp of Anishinabeg. Animals came to the stream, too, and he would be able to build a fish trap. With the stream he had a source of food, water, and a possible way home.

Chickadee followed the stream for days. Sure enough, it widened. It passed through a small lake and he picked up its path on the other side. Always, when he made his night camp, he thanked the chickadee and sang the song it had taught him. Many times, as he walked, he heard the chickadee in the bushes. Sometimes the chickadee perched near him and sang its spring song or scolded in a friendly way, but always in the language of birds. Never again did the little bird speak in a voice that he could understand.

Perhaps it was because I was so weak and helpless, thought Chickadee. *Perhaps my namesake then had pity on me, and the hawks also, though they needed my help.*

Once, as he walked along the stream's edge, a plump gopher dropped from the sky and nearly hit him on the head. He saw the sun through the red tail of a hawk as it disappeared beyond some tall pines.

SEVENTEEN

THE CART TRAIN

The stream widened into a river, and as that river grew there appeared beside it a well-worn trail. When Chickadee came to the trail, he looked from one side to the other as far as he could see. There was no one, and nothing. But the trail was beaten smooth in spite of the spring rains and melting snow. Chickadee had his doubts about taking the road. On the one hand, he could walk it easily and make good time, heading north. On the other hand, so could enemies, and he'd already been kidnapped twice.

Chickadee thought back on the short time since he'd been kidnapped. It had seemed endless! He'd been a servant; he'd eaten miserable bouyah; he'd been painfully scrubbed; his braids were nearly cut off. Chickadee decided that he didn't want to meet other people anymore. Not until he saw his family.

Walking beside the trail, out of sight, was much more difficult, but a better idea altogether. So that's what Chickadee did. When he stopped to sleep, he took a good look up and down the trail to make sure there was no one on it, friend or foe.

As he made his way through the brush and woods, alongside the trail, Chickadee surprised himself by finding food and staying warm. He had the striker and flint for fire, and the knife he'd stolen from the priest. He had thoughts of his family, and the protection of his name-sake, the chickadee. Whenever sad thoughts came over him, or loneliness seized him, he stopped and listened. He always heard the chickadee's cheerful call, urging him on, and his heart lifted.

Again, and again, he sang the chicka-dee's song. He wore the hawk feathers, gifts of his fierce mothers, in his hair.

So Chickadee survived.

He dug cattail roots and roasted them, or ate them raw. He found a rabbit trail and set a snare on it. He waited patiently near the snare, caught a rabbit, and ate that too. He stole eggs from blackbird nests and trapped a fish swimming in the shallows. He ate turtle meat and fashioned himself a little cup from birchbark, which he filled with water. He heated up a stone in his fire and put it into the cup. The water grew very hot. He put in balsam needles and had tea. How comforting it was to drink it. The tea reminded him of Nokomis and her medicines.

There were holes in Chickadee's moccasins now, and his pants were in tatters. His vest kept him warm even in the rain, but the elbows of his shirt were worn out. His elbows stuck out of the sleeves of his shirt. He could see his knees and ankles sometimes as he walked.

How long will I be on this trail? he wondered. *Will I grow into a man as I walk?*

And then something happened.

One day, as he made his way through brush along the trail, he heard something in the distance that he'd never heard before.

It began with a musical creaking that seemed to come from the sky far beyond the trail. Startled, Chickadee crept into some bushes beside the beaten track. He craned out to see down the road as far as he could. There was nothing, and yet little by little the noise increased.

From a songlike creaking it became an off-key squealing. From a squealing it became a squalling. From a squalling it became a screeching, and grew louder. From a bawling screech it became a roaring screech. From a roaring screech it became a deafening shrillness. Just when Chickadee's fright at the sound became panic, he saw an oxcart, the first in a long row.

The ox, the animal that drew the cart, was small, powerful, dark, and tough. It was shaggy and brown with a white spot on its brow. The cart had enormous wheels and it moved shakily but steadily along, lurching and swaying. This cart was the first of two hundred oxcarts in a long line, all piled high with furs and pemmican, dried meat, even quilled pouches and baskets. Some carts were drawn by ponies. The wheels made the screeching sound. A man in a blue shirt, the cart driver, sat in the cart, his feet hanging down right behind the ox. His whip flicked out occasionally, and smoke drifted up out of his pipe. As the cart came closer, Chickadee saw that it was loaded behind with pressed bundles. He knew that these bundles were made up of furs.

The oxcart train was bound from the northern fur country, down through the plains and woods, to St. Paul, Minnesota. In that city, the furs would be bought by fur buyers and sent to New York City. There, they would be sold again to fur buyers from France, England, Germany. There were tons of furs on the Red River oxcart train. Each fur was from an animal trapped or hunted down by an Anishinabe man or woman. Each animal skin was stretched out and preserved, usually by Anishinabe mothers and grandmothers.

Chickadee had never seen so many furs all at once. He

had never seen so many carts! One or two at a time, maybe. Never so many in a row!

The carts made this unbearable noise because they were made entirely of wood. Although bear and buffalo tallow was used on the wheels to make them turn more smoothly, the grease did nothing to keep down the noise. Some of the drivers put plugs of wax in their ears. Others had already gone half deaf.

From his hiding place, Chickadee watched the oxcarts pass. He watched with his fingers stuck firmly in his ears, and his jaw hanging wide. There was a strange and beautiful assortment of people in the carts. One man wore a blue coat with a beautiful ribbon-trimmed hood. There were checkered, calico, plaid, flannel, and wool shirts—all brightly colored. Fancy fringe, beaded shoulder bags, finger-woven red sashes, and every sort of scarf and hat. Some carts were driven by women, who had open parasols tied to shelter against the sun. A few older children ran beside the carts and little children peeped out of the furs. Pots, long-handled frying pans, tipi poles, extra skins, and guns were tied to the sides of some carts and added their clanking to the general din.

Chickadee watched each cart, mesmerized. He wanted to jump out and show himself, to beg for a handout. But he was afraid he would be sent back to the Mother, Sisters, and Father. Or to Babiche and Batiste. He didn't know which was worse. That day, he happened to be particularly hungry. He was so hungry that he'd contemplated eating the tadpoles he saw swimming back in some sloughs he passed. He'd never eaten tadpoles before, and wondered how bad they might taste. Now he decided it would be better to eat tadpoles than hail down an oxcart and be returned to captivity.

But there! All of a sudden! Chickadee took his fingers out of his ears and yelled:

"Uncle!"

Uncle Quill had beeswax plugs in his ears, but he would not have heard Chickadee yell anyway. The oxcarts' din was so tremendous it shook the air. Chickadee had to jump out of his hiding place and run to the cart, and even then, he had to tap his uncle on the toe of his moccasin before he looked down.

Quill was so surprised he nearly fell over in the cart. But Quill was also the sort of man who is not surprised about being surprised. With one neat motion, still holding onto the ox's reins and whip with one hand, he reached down with the other and plucked Chickadee off the ground and hauled him over the pole side of the cart. Quill set his nephew right next to him. He grinned. Uncle Quill had big white teeth and when he smiled the world looked like a better place immediately. Quill knew how to deal with a starving boy, because he'd been one himself and never forgot it. He handed over a flask of water, a bag of pemmican, a hunk of bannock, and he took a piece of beeswax out of his pocket, too.

Chickadee took a drink of water, put the beeswax in his ears, and then proceeded to eat bite after bite of the bannock and handful after handful of delicious pounded berries and buffalo meat. As he filled himself up, sitting there secure next to his uncle, he felt a huge wave of happiness and good luck course over him. He grinned into the distance. Although Chickadee didn't know where he was going, he knew he was with his wonderful uncle, Quill, who loved adventure, was taking him along, and would eventually return him to his family.

EIGHTEEN

RED RIVER TRAIL

Nobody knew about Chickadee's luck back home, of course. Omakayas still woke every morning with Chickadee in her prayers. Mikwam, Yellow Kettle, Nokomis, and all of Chickadee's relatives put pinches of tobacco out and prayed for him too. Makoons tried to be very, very good so that nothing he might do would anger the spirits. He wanted his brother back desperately.

And his father and Two Strike kept walking until they came to the cabin that belonged to Babiche and Batiste.

"Here," said Animikiins. "My son's footprints."

He ran to the ramshackle cabin. It was anything but the cozy place Babiche had described, and Animikiins's heart filled with fear. The cabin was empty.

"Here's the stinking cabin, empty," he called.

"And here," said Two Strike, looking into the stall, "two sad horses, hungry."

Brownie and Brownie had taken to eating the poles of their barn. The poles were now as frail as sticks. The horses would have eaten their way out to the haystack in another day if Animikiins and Two Strike hadn't found them. The horses were dejected and skinny, and when Two Strike released them they went straight for the haystack and began to eat.

"Don't let them eat too much," said Animikiins. "They'll get sick."

Two Strike lured them back to the stall with clumps of hay and let them nibble more carefully.

Animikiins was disgusted by the smell and look of the cabin, and he walked back out to examine the yard. He read the tracks just like white persons read books. He could see the story plainly in the tracks. He soon found that a wagon had stopped, that white women had jumped down. He knew what their tracks looked like with the pointy toe and heel. He saw white man's shoes and his son's tracks again. Then his son's tracks disappeared and the horse and wagon tracks went on.

"He is with these people," said Animikiins. "Whoever they are, they took him. At least he is alive."

Two Strike fed Brownie and Brownie each a lump of maple sugar. The two horses quickly took a liking to her and she had no trouble saddling them up. They were eager to get away from their stall and once Animikiins and Two Strike started out, they galloped along in sudden happiness. The wagon tracks were easy to follow. Brownie and Brownie were used to going places far and fast. They'd grown up hunting buffalo and then delivering the mail. They had big and heroic hearts, gentle dispositions, and stubborn allegiances. They had never been fond of Babiche and Batiste, but they immediately decided that they would obey Two Strike forever.

It took them only two days to track down the wagon—there it was, sitting in a yard. A nun—for Animikiins had seen nuns before—was sweeping the earth in front of a little cabin. There was a cross over the doorway.

Two Strike jumped off Brownie and strode to the nun.

"Where is the boy?" Two Strike asked in Ojibwe.

Sister Seraphica smiled, then looked at the knives in Two Strike's belt. The smile dropped off her face. She looked worried.

"Where is our boy?" asked Animikiins, who spoke some English.

He put his hand out at Chickadee's height.

"Boy," he said again.

"Gone!" said Seraphica.

Mother Anthony came into the doorway behind her.

"Not only gone, but he stole a knife from us!"

Two Strike didn't understand the Mother's language, but she knew that the woman had made an accusation. Two Strike growled fiercely and stuck her face close to the women.

Mother Anthony gave a little scream and disappeared back into the cabin.

Seraphica stayed put.

"He ran away," said Seraphica. "He was a good boy, and Mother Anthony, ah . . . upset him. He ran into the woods. I think he was going home."

Animikiins despaired. He looked at the trees and brush, at the woods that would become great pines and extend on into the great northern forests. Once Chickadee entered the woods, there was no way of finding his trail. Animikiins knew that his son was clever, and for his size he was a strong boy, but could he survive alone in the wild woods? There were so many dangers, not the least of them other humans.

"There is nothing to do, but look and look," he told Two Strike.

With bitter, sinking hearts, the two led the horses into the forest looking for signs of Chickadee. Animikiins was such a good tracker that even after days had passed, he could pick up a trail. He tried, and found signs. Broken plants here, a nest where Chickadee had slept, a place where he'd dug for roots, a little fire pit, places where he'd used his knife to cut bark for tea. The bones of rabbits, the hollowed-out shell of a turtle. They saw he was following a river, and Animikiins smiled.

"He knows how to live," he said proudly, pointing at a lean-to shelter and a scorched place where his son had made a fire.

"This boy is a true Anishinabe," Two Strike agreed.

Animikiins used all his skills. But the earth is good at swallowing up all traces of people. At last, in spite Animikiins's great powers, they lost his trail.

NINETEEN

UNCLE QUILL

Chickadee tried to sleep underneath a Red River cart. He was curled in a buffalo robe next to his Uncle Quill. Draped with buffalo skins, the cart became a snug tent with plenty of room underneath. It was a moonless night, the air was fresh and cool, and Chickadee was warmly wrapped. Uncle Quill slept silently. His breath whooshed evenly, in and out. It was surprising how quiet the carts were once evening fell; the ponies and oxen set about grazing, and everyone made camp.

Of course, at some distance away, there was a party of Metis people laughing around a fire. Quill loved fun and would have stayed up late with them, telling stories and learning their songs. But tonight Quill had felt that his little nephew needed to sleep, and he'd turned in early with Chickadee.

Chickadee should have slept, he was exhausted. He could feel the tiredness creep through his bones and his head was fuzzy with sleep. But Chickadee couldn't quite fall asleep. First of all, there was the sound of musical crying. He'd never heard it before, and he kept sitting up, his ears open. He heard the sound of people singing to the crying music that sometimes skipped and sometimes wailed. Even when he did doze off, Chickadee kept waking up out of dreams in which he was home, with Makoons. He woke with a start, longing for his brother, disoriented and fearful.

At last the music and the voices fell silent. Way off across the distant roll of prairie, wolves howled. An owl glided over and dove for a mouse. One squeak, and it was over. The grass rustled in the wind. Chickadee nestled deeper into the buffalo robe. The fluffy thick fur surrounded him and he began to dream once more. In his dream he saw the buffalo, not just one, but thousands of them. Buffalo thundering across the plains. Buffalo everywhere, coming at him, so thick that they reached to the horizon. He was with them suddenly, running with the herd. Makoons was running too! They were on horses, alongside buffalo, floating and galloping, pounding into darkness and sleep.

• • •

The next morning Chickadee could hardly stir.

"Wake up, little nephew," said Uncle Quill.

Chickadee's mind was sunk in sleep now. After so many nights on bare ground, cold and hungry, the buffalo robe was so comfortable that once he fell asleep, his body wanted to stay asleep. Quill shook his shoulder.

"I brought you tea and bannock," said Quill. "Get up, get in the cart."

Chickadee rolled over and tried to get to his feet, but fell over. He was so sleepy that Uncle Quill lifted him into the cart and nestled him back into the robe. There, Chickadee sat as the oxcart train began to move. He nibbled the bannock and drank the hot brewed black tea, sweetened with maple sugar, from Quill's tin cup. The terrible screeching of the wheels started again and Chickadee put the plugs of wax back into his ears. For that first day, he dozed on and off as the cart slowly made its way along the trail. It was as though he had been in another world, out in the woods, and had to sleep his way into the new world of the oxcarts and Uncle Quill.

At last, when the cool sun was halfway up in the sky, Chickadee crept over to sit beside his uncle. And there they rode. Folded blankets cushioned their bottoms, a comfortable strap made of buffalo hide was tied so they could lean back against it. No sound that they made could penetrate the vast screech in which they moved, so they tried to communicate through signs. There wasn't much they could say yet with signs—that would come later. Mostly they sat companionably together, jouncing back and forth as the cart rolled across the ruts and over the holes in the Red River Trail.

The days and nights began to blur. Their oxcart broke down once, splitting an axle. Uncle Quill cut a new poplar axle from a nearby tree, and lashed it into place with wet strips of buffalo hide. As the strips dried, they shrank, fixing the axle firmly into place. Quill and Chickadee got right back into the train an hour later. Every piece of the cart was made ingeniously of local materials—wood, hide, rope—and could be repaired along the way. There was no metal in the cart, which turned out to be a very good thing one night, as they waited out a lightning storm in some high bare hills.

Although the heavens raged and the rain poured down in sheets, Chickadee and Quill were dry and warm underneath the cart. Lightning struck down everywhere, crashing so hard the earth shook. The oxen were slightly worried but very tired, too, and merely slept with heads bent under the driving rain.

"We are safe from the thunderbirds under these carts," said Quill. "They love biwabik, you know, things of metal. When the U.S. cavalry comes out on the Plains with its

iron tent poles, the thunderbirds amuse themselves by striking them!"

Quill knew lots of things. He told Chickadee about the people with the colorful clothing.

"They are Metis. They are the sons and daughters of the French and Anishinabe and Cree all mixed together. My Deydey, your grandfather, knows how to talk with them. Listen to the way they speak! They mix all of the languages into one language. After a while you'll pick it right up, as I have."

"They sing French songs," said Chickadee.

"Their fathers taught them songs from the days when they paddled canoes. Before these trails, that was the only way to carry furs! I remember it!"

"What are those crying instruments they play?"

"Those are fiddles. You'll see."

"And their clothing—it is all colors and yet some is like ours."

"They like to wear moccasins. Who would ever want to wear white men's shoes? But the women wear big skirts. The men wear blouses. They like some of our clothes. We like some of theirs."

"Why do you know so much about these people, Uncle Quill?"

"Because I am married to one!"

Chickadee was silent. He had forgotten that his uncle had married. Chickadee was out of questions.

The next day, as Uncle Quill brewed tea and fried some bannock on a little fire, a Metis woman came up to him and began to talk in her language. Quill answered her, and Chickadee tried to make out what they were saying. He caught a few words here and there—it sounded like they were talking about him. The woman made gestures all about herself, slapping her knee, rubbing her elbow. Chickadee realized that she was describing the rips and tears in his clothing. Quill was smiling and nodding now. The woman left.

"She's going to make you a new shirt, new moccasins, and fix your pants and vest," he said. "She said such a nice-looking boy as you shouldn't be dressed so poor."

"Am I dressed so poor?"

Chickadee looked down at his clothing, and noticed the rips and tears and spots of grease he'd gotten used to.

"Yes, I guess I look pretty bad, my uncle."

"Your mama would have fixed you up by now. But your Uncle Quill can't do much."

The woman came back and made Chickadee stand still. She took a piece of sinew and measured his feet, his arms, his chest. She took his vest away and fixed it that very afternoon. When she brought it back, the woolen vest had been cleaned. The rips were neatly sewn, and where there had been holes she had cleverly beaded on circles of hide. Two days later, the woman brought back a shirt of bright blue calico. It had wide sleeves and a collar that peeked from the vest. She took away his old shirt and fixed that too, and by adding more fringe and pieces of tanned deerhide, she made it into a jacket. New moccasins came next. Chickadee gave up his pants overnight and in the morning she brought them back, all repaired and with a piece of hide stitched around the bottom so that his ankles were covered.

"I look so fine," said Chickadee.

He was delighted with himself, and the woman could tell, and laughed. She had big white teeth in her round face and wore lots of bead necklaces. Her braids were gray when they came unbound from her neat bun. As she walked, her skirt swirled around her quick steps. Her name was French, Antoinette. She had two children—her grandchildren—with her, and they were well dressed too. Antoinette had her own cart. Her granddaughter drove it; the other child, a small boy, usually walked beside the ox and kept an eye out for game he might catch.

After she made Chickadee's new clothing, Quill invited them to hitch their ox to the back of his cart. That way the young driver could take a rest once in a while, as Quill kept the animals moving. And so the pack train went on and on until a small river stopped them.

The flood and force of the river had dissipated, and it was a mild flow now, though broad. There was no ferry. There was no way to cross it except to change their versatile carts into boats.

This was being done all up and down the river, as each cart and driver reached the banks.

To Chickadee's surprise, he saw that some carts were already in the water, floating across. Uncle Quill and another man worked together. First they wrenched off the wheels and lashed them together. Then they dismantled the carts and used the poles for siding so the baggage would not slide off into the water. The oxen and horses would swim across, and Uncle Quill and Chickadee would swim too, holding on to the poles and attempting to guide the raft.

Uncle Quill helped Antoinette to transform her cart, too, and one after the next the little cart train forded the river. The river was still very cold, and on the other side fires were quickly made to dry out clothing and warm numb fingers. The oxen and horses shook themselves and lowered their heads to graze. The sun was so low by the time all of the carts had crossed that everyone made camp on the banks of the river.

That night, the fiddle playing was extra lively, and Antoinette and her grandchildren invited Chickadee to join in the fun. Uncle Quill already knew the Red River jig, and he shouted with joy, dancing with the rest of the men. Chickadee caught the spirit and the flames leaped high. The fiddles wailed and jumped. Antoinette danced like a young woman, kicking up her skirts, her white teeth gleaming in the firelight.

"Here is how we jig, little Chickadee," she called, and her small feet in pretty moccasins flashed fast in fancy steps.

As Chickadee watched, he remembered how his mother danced and clapped when she was happy. He remembered how Zozie trilled like a bird when she was excited, how his father played his beautiful hand drum and joyously sang a traveling song or a hunting song. Most of all, he remembered how Makoons jumped up and down, threw his head back, and laughed so hard he fell on the ground and rolled when things were too funny to bear. His chest swelled with confusion. If only his twin were here! He was happy, he was going home, eventually, someday. But could he stand it? Could he wait to see his brother? How long would it be?

TWENTY

MAKOONS

Ever since his father and Two Strike had returned, with news that they had lost Chickadee's trail, Makoons had begun to feel the strangeness of his life. One morning, fishing for goldeneyes as usual, he fell into the cold Red River. He let the current take him downstream quite a way before he roused himself, panicked, and swam wildly for the shore.

After that, Makoons just felt wrong. It was the chill, Nokomis thought, and she dosed him with many cups of thick black tea. He had a cough, which she treated with boiled cherrybark. His chest hurt. Nokomis put a plaster of steaming lily-pad root right over his heart. Makoons cried at the sting of heat, but his chest cleared. Still, he dragged from place to place and could hardly manage to set one foot before the other on some days. When he sat down, he leaned over, closed his eyes, and quickly fell asleep. When he woke, it was to the sad memory of his brother's absence.

Omakayas was worried.

"Come here, my boy," she said gently. "Sit with me. We are missing your brother, aren't we?"

"Yes," said Makoons.

"Let us sit here and think about him then," said Omakayas. Tears came into her eyes.

"I know he is alive," Makoons said. "I feel his presence. I know he's looking for us."

"He is strong and he will find us," said Omakayas. "We have to be patient and wait."

Makoons looked at her helplessly. Waiting was very hard. It was so difficult to stay in one place waiting for your twin, the other half of you, to show up. Any moment he might appear. Or he might not appear. There was no certainty. That's what was hardest. That's what tired him.

Makoons crept next to his mother, lay against her. Exhaustion crept over him. The chill from the river came back and he shivered, even though the day was warm. His mother made tea from wild rose hips, covered him with a blanket. Omakayas sang to him and stroked his hair until he slept. She was very worried.

"Nokomis," she said when her grandmother appeared. "We need to make another, better, strengthening tea for Makoons. We have to feed him well. We must keep him from growing ill."

"I know," said Nokomis. "I, too, am worried that he could pine away for his twin. I am going out to gather medicines, plant food, and watch the horizon. One day, from that distance, I know our boy will appear."

Nokomis took her bean seeds from the little pouch she had carried across Minnesota. Even when most of their things had been stolen, she'd saved a few seeds. She loved to make gardens, and had a nose for whom to ask for seeds. She'd added to those few seeds with others that she traded for from the people of Garden Island, in Lake of the Woods. All around that great and complicated lake, there had been women who planted corn, gourds, beans.

Now, bending over the soft earth, Nokomis took a few bean seeds and carefully buried them. She marked each seed with a tall stick. She worked the fish bones, the heads and fins and scales, into the soil between the seeds. Then she carried water in a wooden bucket to each one. It used to be, she reflected, that she could make a new container from birchbark any time she wanted. She just had to find a tree, remove the bark, and fashion her vessel. Nokomis sighed at the memory. On the Plains, there were few birch trees. And even those few had thin and crinkly skin. They made frail baskets, and terrible buckets. This one wooden bucket had to do a lot of work. It was the only one they had.

Angeline and Yellow Kettle straightened their backs. They were planting seed potatoes given to them by Father Belcourt. At that same moment, using a saw borrowed from the priest, and hinges traded for with maple sugar, Mikwam and Fishtail were making a little trapdoor in the wood floor of the cabin. They were digging out a root cellar, anticipating that there would be potatoes to keep there by fall. They were hauling sand to line the bottoms of the bins—they had learned that this trick kept the potatoes and squash at the right temperature all winter.

After the cellar was dug and the door finished off with a rope handle, the two went out to work on the pole fences. They had put to use old poles left behind, setting them in place between shorter logs pounded into the earth. They now had a small fenced yard, and a shanty for Brownie and Brownie to shelter inside when the rain poured. Otherwise the horses were tough and grazed the grasses all around on staked lines. Their bellies grew, though one Brownie's belly was growing bigger than the other's.

Zozie had joined Nokomis in the garden. She pointed at the horses and said, "Nokomis, I think one of the Brownies is going to have a foal."

"You're right," said Nokomis, nodding happily. "It won't be long. We are lucky that Two Strike knows what to do."

Two Strike, who had taken charge of the horses, cared for them religiously. At night, she slept near them in a pile of sweet, dry grass. By day, she worked and trained them. She practiced riding, along with Animikiins. As soon as possible, they planned to take those two horses and hunt buffalo. They were making friends among the other Anishinabeg, and also among the Metis who lived all around the town and up into the low hills. Once the Red River carts returned and the families were again together, they would follow the buffalo off into the Plains and hunt them to fill those carts again.

They would use each part of the buffalo and build up their winter stores of dried meat. They would make pemmican, tan hides, make beautiful fluffy robes, and keep the horns to make powder carriers, knife handles, spoons, even buttons and tobacco boxes. How Two Strike looked forward to that hunt.

But even as Two Strike made plans, Animikiins fell silent. His heart was heavy. He worked as hard as he could. But waiting and wondering about Chickadee weighed so heavy on his heart, sometimes, that he couldn't breathe. There were times when he sat with Omakayas, holding her hand, neither of them saying a word hour after hour. How could they go on? Yet they did go on, waiting for their son.

TWENTY-ONE

ST. PAUL

The oxcart train jogged and wobbled, in a sea of noise, down a path that became a wide road. This road broadened and smoothed itself out and at last became a series of streets lined with wooden buildings. Chickadee sat beside Uncle Quill and looked with amazement at the ornamented tops of the buildings. There were many log cabins and many more plank houses, too. For which reason, of course, there was not a tree in sight. The signs that marked the glass windows of the stores were bright and bold. The people walked on wooden paths and stared at the oxcarts and held their hands over their ears.

148

The muddy path took them along the river, where each cart would unload. As the cart jounced along, Chickadee stared up at the bluff above the river.

Towering high over the slope he saw the biggest houses in the world. They were carved of trees. Each was of a different shape and color. Great windows like staring eyes glared over the river. Doors like mouths swung open as people came out, drawn by the outrageous noise of the oxcarts. The people stood high on the bluff, shading their eyes, pointing

down at the carts and the drivers and the children, who shaded their eyes, too, and pointed right back up at them.

It was not polite to point. Nokomis had always stopped Chickadee from pointing at a person.

"You are stabbing at that person's spirit," she had told Chickadee. "And never point at clouds because there might be a thunderbird up there, or at the water because you must not challenge water, or at the islands because they are also alive."

Nokomis pointed by puckering her lips and nodding at whatever she wanted to indicate. Most other Anishinabeg did too.

Chickadee had rarely pointed at anything or anybody in his life. But he was so astonished at those houses, which Uncle Quill called mansions, that he pointed right up at them, and nobody stopped him.

Uncle Quill just smiled at his nephew's surprise. He'd been in St. Paul before.

The oxcart train made camp by a lake.

Although he was excited to be in St. Paul, he also wanted to go home. He looked at the ground. One hawk feather, blown by the wind and trampled by passing carts, stuck raggedly out of the mud. Chickadee plucked it out of the road and carefully tucked it into his shirt. There weren't very many birds in St. Paul, but one of his helpers had passed over.

One by one, each cart was unloaded at the trader's

warehouse. The bales of fur were weighed, their quality assessed. The horn spoons and bowls, the baskets and quilled shirts were bargained for. Antoinette sold seven pairs of embroidered moccasins and eight calico shirts that she'd made on the way. She was such a quick and clever seamstress that she'd make as many on the way back and sell another batch in Pembina.

Once a cart had been emptied, it would then be reloaded with things that people back home had requested from the St. Paul traders. The people up north, around Pembina, needed metal dishes, bolts of wool and calico, rifles, ammunition, ribbons, beads, door latches, bucket handles, ingots of metal, and reams of paper. Tar paper, writing paper, wrapping paper, oil paper were loaded into the carts. There were lanterns and lantern oil. Coffeepots. Coffee beans. Tea. Sugar. Flour. Nails. Hammers. Delicate windows. Packets of bright candy.

All of these things and more!

As they waited at the end of the line for their cart to be assessed, Chickadee watched everything around him. He saw his uncle squint hard at the line of traders who were bargaining for each load. The traders wore fancy vests, boots with a harsh shine quickly covered with mud and dust, and white shirts. They had loud, excited voices that dropped to a whisper as they decided on prices. Each had a pad of paper on which he wrote out numbers. Still squinting hard,

Chickadee saw his uncle pull a pad of paper and a long pointed feather out of a packet at his elbow. He also had a little bottle filled with a black substance. Uncle Quill dipped his sharpened feather into the ink, and began to scratch it across his paper.

The traders Uncle Quill had been looking at approached the wagon and gave out a huge guffaw.

"Looka here, this savage is *writin'*!"

Several of the other traders craned to see what was going on. Uncle Quill continued calmly to dip his pen in the bottle and to make signs on the paper. Two more traders came over to see what was happening and gawked at the sight of Uncle Quill, who occasionally brushed his forehead with the tip of the feather and looked into the clouds, as if for inspiration.

"Whatcha writin'?" asked one of the traders.

Quill glanced at them through his shaggy hair, then handed over the paper. The first trader read out the numbers on the paper, then frowned. Another trader jostled him, took the paper, and wrote another number down beside Quill's number. Still another trader looked at everything in the cart, grabbed the paper, and wrote down yet another number and handed it up to Quill before a fourth trader could elbow his way over. Quill looked at the number and shrugged. He waited for the last trader to make his way to the cart, and handed the paper to him. The last trader kicked one of the other traders in the knee, wrote down a number quickly, tossed the pad of paper up to Quill.

Quill read the number, thought a moment, then nodded. The other traders turned their attention to the other carts. Quill followed this trader to his warehouse, where money was counted out to him. Once Quill had counted and recounted the coins, he allowed his cart to be unloaded.

After the quick unloading came the next part of the exchange. Quill and Chickadee went to the storeroom next to the trader's fur warehouse.

When Chickadee walked into the storeroom, his mouth dropped open. There were bags upon bags of flour, sugar, meal, oats. There were tins of tea and jars of red-and-white-striped sticks. Bales of calico and wool, boxes of dried fruit and salted meats. There were tin buckets and stacks of animal traps. Knives of every size and shape.

"Here, boy," said the trader. He handed Chickadee a striped stick. It was a nice stick. Chickadee looked at it. He'd never seen a stick like this before. He waved it through the air. He tapped it on his hand.

Uncle Quill laughed.

"Taste it," he said.

Chickadee put the red-and-white stick in his mouth. His eyes opened wide as the sweetness and deliciousness of the peppermint struck his tongue with a blow of joy.

He took the stick out with a wild smile.

"Uncle," he cried. "Minopogwad! It tastes *good*!"

Uncle Quill laughed again and then proceeded to bargain with the goods agent until he had what he needed loaded back into the cart.

As Uncle Quill was bargaining, Chickadee slowly enjoyed his first taste of candy. But as he tasted it with every fiber of his being, he thought of Makoons and wished that his brother could be eating a peppermint stick too. When he had licked and nibbled the stick exactly halfway down, Chickadee wrapped it in a stray piece of paper that a trader had dropped on the floor. Then he put the peppermint in the same pouch where he kept his striker. He would keep it for his brother. If only he could give it to Makoons right this minute!

Finally, the last decisions were made and the merchandise was piled near the cart. Chickadee and Uncle Quill secured everything with ropes and covered their precious cargo with the buffalo hides kept to protect the wares on the way back.

That night, as the oxcart train made camp near the outskirts of the city, Chickadee saw the flicker of candlelight and lamplight high on the hill where the great houses stood. He wondered if he would ever see the inside of one of those houses whose great windows blared sheaves of light. They made huge blurred spears that reached out into the balmy spring darkness. He heard voices up there, tinkly music, and the clatter of hoofbeats as carriages and wagons rolled over wooden planks and stone pathways. He thought of Makoons again. Could he ever convey this sight in words? He would have to memorize all that he was seeing so that he could tell his brother of what was there. Only his brother would understand, he thought, the black uneasiness that he also felt.

It seemed to Chickadee that those houses held the powers of the world. The ones who built and lived in those houses were making an outsize world. An existence he'd never dreamed of. Almost a spirit world, but one on earth. Chickadee could see that they used up forests of trees in making the houses. He could see that they had cut down every tree in sight. He could feel that they were pumping up the river and even using up the animals. He thought of the many animals whose dead hides were bound and sold in St. Paul in one day. Everything that the Anishinabeg counted on in life, and loved, was going into this hungry city mouth. This mouth, this city, was wide and insatiable. It would never be satisfied, thought Chickadee dizzily, until everything was gone.

That night, Chickadee tried to sleep. But he was too excited to drop off into slumber. There was a loud uproar around the fire, and Chickadee decided to watch the dancing and listen to the fiddle music. People from St. Paul were so happy to see relatives from the oxcart train that they brought out extra food. There were many fiddle players sitting on stumps, playing together or taking turns. As they played, they kept time with their feet. The firelight gleamed across their bright eyes and they played with joy and effort, squeezing up their mouths and bending up and down as they came to the quickest parts of their songs.

And the dancers! Chickadee now realized that the dancing he'd seen on the way to St. Paul was nothing compared with a real Metis celebration! The men were dressed in their best clothes—stocking caps, fancy berets with round pompoms, brimmed hats, striped hats! Their shirts were dripping with ribbons and fringe, and they wore long red sashes, finger-woven like the carrying straps that Nokomis made.

The women were even brighter. Necklaces of every color of bead glistened and bounced as they jigged. Their full skirts bounced around their ankles, showing fancy underskirts and colored stockings. Their moccasins, like those of the men, were beaded with intricate flowers. Their hair was held up in silver pins or braided tightly with ribbons or swung loose and free as they whirled and tapped. Their feet moved so fast sometimes that they seemed to blur. And all the time they were laughing, the men were smiling, the children were tumbling about, their mouths smeared with food, their eyes brilliant.

Chickadee saw Antoinette in a jigging contest with another woman. Each did her fancy steps to the fiddle, and then held out a hand to let the other jig. The men clapped and urged them on with delighted cries. And the fiddles never stopped. Sometimes they squeaked high and fast. Sometimes they groaned low. Sometimes they brought every-one to their feet. Sometimes, when a fiddler let loose with a wild air, the dancers stopped to clap and encourage the fiddler to greater effort.

All of a sudden, Chickadee saw Uncle Quill leap into the middle of the circle. He did not have on fancy clothes, beadwork, a hat, or red leggings. But his footwork was so fast and dainty and his jigging so precise that Chickadee was amazed. Then he disappeared. Other men took his place. The whirl of music and dancing went on for hours and Chickadee finally could not keep his eyes open for even one more song. He stumbled back to the wagon, crept beneath the cart and fell asleep even as the Metis people danced, laughed, and drank until dawn.

The first carts started moving while the sky was still faintly pink. Chickadee crawled sleepily into the oxcart and snuggled up in the buffalo robe behind his uncle. He checked his pouch to make sure that the half peppermint stick was still there. It was safe. Chickadee dozed off as the cart began its familiar jouncing. He opened his eyes once and smiled, knowing that every turn of the wheel brought him closer now to his twin.

• • •

Life had sprung up along the trail. The thin film of green in the trees had become a cloud of new leaves. Robins, bluebirds, vireos, finches, songbirds of all types made the brush along the trail a wall of sharp melody. The broad road went on and on and the traveling was very pleasant. Off to the side of the road there were houses, and every so often there was a town to stop at, a settlement where Quill occasionally made a purchase. At one place he added to the ribbons he'd bought for his wife by buying a hat straight off a woman's head. At another place, he bought a pie. He cut it down the middle and he and Chickadee ate it right there.

Alongside the road, the number of sloughs increased as they left behind farmland and journeyed toward the forest. The road narrowed, then it got bumpy, and filled with stumps that could break an axle. There were rocks, branches, mud holes, twisting roots. In the sloughs, high-pitched spring peepers and deep-throated bullfrogs joined in a chorus so loud it could even be heard above the squeak of wheels. Eagles, hawks, herons, and great flocks of ducks wheeled down and clattered up into the sky as the oxcart train passed.

But of course along with the sparkling sounds of birds and the delicious dinners of duck, spring brought newly hatched mosquitoes. As they left the flat plains and ventured on up into forest and prairie lands, the mosquitoes found them.

First, it was a slap here, a bite there, but a smudge fire in the night would drive them from the sleeping area. Then things got worse. The insects seemed to be everywhere. At last, one afternoon on a rolling piece of prairie dotted with wildflowers, a spot so pretty that even a young boy would admire it, Chickadee saw a dark cloud wavering ahead. There was no wind. All was still. The cloud gave him an uneasy feeling. He asked his uncle what it was, but Quill didn't answer. When Chickadee glanced at him to see if he'd heard, he saw that Quill's face was contorted by an expression he'd never seen there. Quill's eyes were open wide, he panted and a small moan escaped his chest.

"Get my jacket, my facecloth, my mitts!"

Chickadee handed these items to his uncle from the bag in the center of the cart.

"Now you get down! Get underneath the robe. Quick!"

Chickadee did as his uncle ordered, as fast as he could. By the time he pulled the robe over his head, he heard a strange, whining, vibrating, terrifying roar. And then the cloud descended.

The attack was unlike anything Chickadee had ever

experienced. He knew what mosquitoes were like, naturally. He knew them all too well. But living near a lake he could escape them by jumping straight in the water. He could cover his body with mud. There were plants his Nokomis smeared on him that the mosquitoes did not like. Out here, there was no place to hide. Everyone was defenseless.

Uncle Quill cried out. The poor oxen bellowed. Millions and millions of mosquitoes landed on the flesh of every living being in the oxcart train. The train became a moving mosquito feast. Children cried, men wept and cursed, and the poor animals, whipped by the drivers and tormented by the insects, groaned as they trudged forward. There was nowhere to go but forward.

There was no wind, no breeze at all, so the mosquitoes could land and attack at will.

Wrapped in the robe, Chickadee got only a few bites at first. But then the biting cloud discovered him too and great bunches of mosquitoes jammed themselves through every opening, stinging ferociously, sucking his blood out of him with thousands of tiny straws.

Chickadee yelled, cried, groaned like the poor oxen, but there was nothing to be done. Every time he smacked away a cluster of mosquitoes, a new ferocious avalanche of them took its place. In a few minutes, he was bitten to pieces. What would happen to him in the hours ahead? He didn't think he could last. Every time he opened his mouth to take a breath, he took a mouthful of mosquitoes in. They filled his nose, his ears. They stung his eyelids, even tried to get his poor eyeballs.

The oxcart train was moving as fast as it could, trying to get through the deadly cloud. The beasts were so thickly covered with insects that there wasn't a scrap of hide visible. They were all gray. That terrible, moving, feeding, sucking gray color of mosquitoes. Crying out with pain, the drivers used their whips again and again. To stop was death. A mosquito cloud like this could literally drain the blood from the oxen and the horses, leaving them too weak to pull the carts. So all that day, in a mindless groaning howl of agony, they plunged along the trail.

By nightfall, there was still no wind, and the mosquitoes were unhindered in their viciousness. The oxcart train stopped, and as quickly as possible smudge fires were lighted. These fires smoked when old leaves and wet branches were added to the flames. The smoke spread over the encampment, and the cloud lifted slightly, hovering just above the smoke, sending down only thousands, not millions, of their number. Uncle Quill covered his ox with a heavy piece of wool. He made the tent underneath the wagon as mosquito tight as he could. He kept a smudge fire going on each side of the cart, getting up every hour to feed it through the night.

It was a tortuous night.

Chickadee thought nothing could get worse than the

attack in the cart, but to fall asleep and then be awakened by the mosquitoes was somehow worse.

"Pray for a wind, or rain, or cold!" said Uncle Quill. "That's all that can drive them off."

Both of them begged for relief before the night was over, but by morning the mosquitoes raged even more harshly as the pack train started out again.

The prairie almost seemed to mock them with its beauty. Every inch of their skin was covered with bites upon bites. Their faces were purple and swollen. The mosquitoes bit through cloth, they bit through hair, they were implacable. Every being suffered. Yet they kept moving.

The sun was high in the sky by the time the mosquitoes began to settle. It was unnoticeable at first, and then slowly—infinitely slowly—the cloud of insects broke up into cruel bands and wavering streams. Eventually, in the heat of the day, a brisk wind rose. The mosquitoes, too light to land in wind, diminished. Then at last there was relief. Sweet relief. Almost too sweet to bear.

TWENTY-TWO

TOUCHING EARTH

Omakayas sat next to her son Makoons, holding his dry hand. He was hot with fever, and lay perfectly still. At least the worst of it was over, and he squeezed her hand back from time to time and sipped cool water or Nokomis's medicine. Nokomis was out foraging for more willow bark. Brewed into a tea, the inner bark helped ease the fever. Makoons was slowly improving, but these days it seemed that no sooner did he get over an illness than he succumbed to another one. Zozie, so good at hunting small game and drying meat, was busy boiling a broth of rabbit and beaver meat. She stirred in dried and pounded cattail root, to thicken the broth. Then she brought a bowl over to

Omakayas. Slowly, she spooned the broth into Makoons's mouth. He swallowed carefully, then fell asleep. Even eating seemed to exhaust him.

"Chickadee, my brother," he mumbled in his sleep. Makoons smiled. He smiled only in his sleep. Omakayas was sure those smiles happened only when he was dreaming of playing with Chickadee.

Zozie put her hand on her second mother's shoulder.

"I know he is alive somewhere," said Omakayas.

"I know it, too," said Zozie.

"I think that I should feel it if my son were gone from this earth," said Omakayas slowly. Inside, she was not so sure. Nobody could understand all that happened on this earth, and Omakayas was not a medicine person yet, not like Nokomis, although her grandmother was teaching her everything she knew.

The little cabin was propped up and stabilized now, and the logs were tightly chinked with mud. The floor was tamped down and then covered with rush mats. Everyone took off their moccasins when entering, so the mats stayed nice and clean. Fishtail had traded for a small square stove, and the wood was neatly stacked beside. He and Angeline had roped off a small room in one corner, hung with blankets and made snug. In another corner, Mikwam and Yellow Kettle slept. Omakayas and Animikiins had their part of the room too. Nokomis curled near the stove with Zozie and Makoons. And Two Strike slept outside with the horses.

Although nine people lived in the tiny cabin, and one outside, there was empty space that could be filled only by Chickadee.

Out in back, the seeds that Nokomis had saved so carefully were now sprouting. The corn leaves were sturdy and fresh. The dark potato leaves curled down from their mounds of earth. Tendrils of squash and bean vines had begun their searching climb up the poles Nokomis sank near each plant. Every day Nokomis, helped by Yellow Kettle, added to the fence around the garden. Fishtail, Animikiins, and Two Strike worked with the horses.

Mikwam was learning how to build a cart. He decided that his canoe-building skills were of little use on the prairie, and he'd best learn from the masters of the Red River cart. When he began building the cart, using borrowed tools, cutting and working the wood, he amazed his family.

"This old man is a wonder," said Yellow Kettle proudly. "He will not be stopped. He is building us a cart!"

"He is making it so that we can join the buffalo hunt," said Two Strike. "We will learn the ways of these Metis people and copy their hunting."

"It is lucky that Babiche and Batiste so kindly gave you their horses," said Fishtail.

"Kindly," said Two Strike. "I'd like to see them kindly try to take them back after stealing our Chickadee."

Makoons came out the door and she fell silent. Two Strike reached out helplessly as Makoons walked by.

"My boy," she said, her harsh voice unusually low and coaxing, "would you like to ride Brownie or Brownie? They have become gentle, obedient, and love you. Look!"

She pointed at the horses, who were tossing their heads up and down. To Makoons it looked like they were agreeing with Two Strike. Actually, they always tossed their heads up and down when they saw Two Strike because she brought them whatever treats she could find. She shared tender plants, sweetened bread, dried berries, and more. The horses believed she was one of them, their leader. Wherever she walked, they followed. When she stopped, they stopped. They stood behind her, craned over her shoulder, and gently lowered their hard noses and velvet lips to her hands.

Makoons looked at them indifferently, but allowed Two Strike to help him into the saddle. Brownie flicked her ears to Two Strike and listened to all she said, then began to trot around and around her in an even circle. As Two Strike turned, the horse kept her eye lovingly on the powerful woman. Slowly, Makoons eased into the horse's stride. Soon, he was cantering along with wonderful ease, his hands caught in Brownie's flowing mane.

"Majaan!" cried Two Strike, sweeping her hands toward the open prairie. Away Brownie loped, Makoons on her back. He actually laughed. He rode the horse into the

distance, and then Two Strike whistled. Brownie flicked
back an ear and headed home. Two Strike had a piece of
jellied bannock waiting. She looked anxiously at Makoons.
His eyes looked brighter, but the moment his feet touched
ground his shoulders sagged.

"If only we could keep him on a horse day and night,
he might get better. You could help him," said Two Strike
to Brownie. "But he is a human. Sometimes he must walk
the same earth as his brother. As soon as his feet touch that
ground, he is reminded that somewhere, nowhere, anywhere, his brother walks too."

TWENTY-THREE

RETURN OF THE BOUYAH

After the mosquitoes, the oxcart train made good time on a level piece of prairie and even managed the difficult part of the road that wound in and out of the woods, through sloughs and alongside quaking bogs. There was plenty of fresh game along the trail, and every night the fiddles came out. Antoinette brewed coffee. The Metis liked to celebrate any small thing that happened, as well as big things. Birthdays were big things, and it seemed to Chickadee that everyone and even the oxen had parties at night for their special days.

The sloughs began to blend together, and the oxen struggled in the mushy ground. One day the carts at the beginning of the line made it through a deep slough, but by the time Uncle Quill's cart—and then Antoinette's, who was just behind them—got to the swampiest place, it was impossible. Both carts sank their wheels right in and could not budge.

Immediately, men from the other carts came to try to extricate the two carts. From firmer ground, they tried to pull the oxen up. From behind, they tried to push the carts. They cut great bunches of reeds and laid them down under the wheels, but the muck seemed bottomless.

In the middle of all the effort, everyone paused to catch a breath. They stood around the stuck carts pondering their next move, arguing and thinking up new advice. As they stood there, Chickadee saw two men approaching. They were coming down the road far ahead, but he recognized them anyway. Though tiny, they were also huge. They slouched along, packs slung across their backs, smoking their pipes, gesturing, laughing. They wore the same knitted red hats, had the same drum-tight bellies, and their beards stuck out to each side ferociously.

"Uncle," said Chickadee, pulling on Quill's sleeve. "Those two men are coming, the two I told you about!"

"Not now," said Quill. He was worried that an axle or wheel might break beneath the strain. Or that the cart would sit in the mud until the middle of summer. He was trying to figure a way out.

"Uncle," said Chickadee, more urgently, "those are the

men who kidnapped me!"

"Eya'," said Quill distractedly. "Maybe we can cut some popple trees and make a little bridge to get those oxen out. I saw some trees a few miles back."

"Remember their names? Babiche and Batiste! They're here."

And they were. Chickadee held tightly to his uncle's jacket. He wasn't exactly afraid that Babiche and Batiste would steal him again, but he wondered what they were up to. He didn't trust them. And their horses were gone. Where were Brownie and Brownie? Why were they on foot?

"Sacre coeur!" bellowed Babiche when he saw Chickadee.

"Our Little Master!" Bastiste cried. "He survived!"

The two great brothers plunged through the slough and rose dripping and happy. They tried to embrace Chickadee, but Quill now remembered the whole story and stood between them and his nephew.

"Your Little Master?" Chickadee was more than surprised. "I was your servant the last time I saw you! What happened?"

"Ah," said Babiche, "my good brother and I had our hearts clarified. We met a great woman. A woman of many knives. A woman stronger than the two of us together. We both asked her to marry us!"

"Two Strike? You asked her to marry you?"

"Awee," said both brothers.

"She is strong enough a wife for both of us," said Batiste.

"We said that we would serve her until we perished. But she said, 'Serve Chickadee instead.'"

"But we didn't know where you were! Oh, Grace of God, now we have found you! You, our Little Master!"

Babiche and Batiste threw their arms wide.

"No need," said Chickadee, and introduced his uncle and then Antoinette and her grandchildren. He asked what had happened to Brownie and Brownie.

"We gave them to the great lady. We gave them as wedding gifts," said Babiche. "May it be true that she still has them and is considering our request!"

"I am sure she's thinking about it," said Uncle Quill. "But we will never know unless we make it out of this mud. It threatens to suck these carts right down to hell!"

"We would never let that happen!" cried Babiche.

"We will use our endless strength!"

The two great brothers rubbed their hands together, and their force was combined with the others who strove in the muddy slough. Slowly, with an endless sucking groan, the first ox was pulled free. Then the brothers put their immense arms to work and lifted the cart right out of the mud and carried it to firm ground. They did the same for Antoinette's oxcart.

"*Mon dieu,*" she exclaimed. "I have never seen such power! You must need food for your great bellies now!"

"Awee, madame, so we do," said the brothers.

The carts labored on for some distance, until the way

looked clear again and they had caught up to the rest of the train. The first carts were already camped, and so Uncle Quill did the same. Antoinette invited the two brothers to camp with her family, and to enjoy her cooking. Chickadee heard Babiche say the word *bouyah*, and he sidled over to his uncle.

"Uncle, have you ever tasted bouyah?" he asked.

Uncle Quill looked down at Chickadee with pity in his eyes.

"Were you forced to eat bouyah?" he asked.

"Yes, my uncle."

"There is some good bouyah," said Quill. "My wife makes it, and I'll bet Antoinette makes a good batch too. But it can be terrible stuff!"

"Geget, I could not agree more. Gidebwe," said Chickadee.

"If Antoinette offers us some supper," said Quill, "and I know she will, we will smell it first. We will test it just a little. I have found it is always wise to be cautious where bouyah is concerned."

That night, the camp rested exhaustedly after the efforts of the day. Passing into slumber, Chickadee heard a pack of wolves howling in the near distance. He could tell that they were howling for joy and thought they were probably celebrating their young pups as they emerged from their dens. Maybe they had made a kill that day, and all of them felt like singing. Their song went on and on into the night, and Chickadee slept happily, his back against his uncle's buffalo robe. When he woke the next morning, a light rain was lashing down all around the cart. Antoinette had fixed a set of bent willow branches on her cart, and when it rained or the sun became too hot, she fastened her canvas tipi over the poles and traveled in comfort.

"My boy," said Uncle Quill, "we are going to do the same."

He had bought some canvas in St. Paul, and now he spotted strong new willow growing near. After drinking some tea at Antoinette's camp, he cut the poles and erected the same contraption on his oxcart.

"Now *this* is traveling," he said happily to Chickadee as they started out. In spite of the rain, they now continued along a ridge of land that was perfectly solid. It was a pleasure to jounce along. The ox was well fed on new grass and pulled easily. The gentle rain blew about them in warm gusts, but they were dry beneath the canvas.

When they talked now, they mainly read each other's lips. With their ears plugged and the appalling creaking of the carts, they couldn't even hear each other yell. But they managed to communicate quite well even so.

"Uncle Quill," said Chickadee as they traveled the good road, "can you tell me a story about when you were young?"

Quill laughed.

"In those days I was always getting into trouble!"

"That's what Mama says."

"She's right. One time I stayed behind on purpose, at wild rice camp. Everybody left without me. I was alone in the woods."

"I know what that's like," said Chickadee.

"It wasn't so bad," said Uncle Quill.

"Did you meet any spirits?"

"Several times, I did. They were memegwesiwag, little people spirits. Once, your mother and I got caught in the rapids. At night! There we were in our canoe, washed right downstream, pushed along quick as an arrow. In the dark! We could see nothing. It's amazing we came out of that alive. But we were protected by the memegwesiwag who lived along that stream. I saw one afterward, a hairy little round man. He was smiling at us. He looked proud that we'd lived."

"I have never seen one of those spirits," said Chickadee. "But when I was alone, starving, two hawks had pity on me because I helped them. Also, I have spoken to my own namesake, and the little bird gave advice to me."

"Ah," said Quill, "you are very fortunate! You must remember that advice forever. Did he give you anything else?"

"A song."

Quill gave a low whistle.

"This is a very powerful thing, my boy. To have your namesake, your protector, and a song. You will be able to heal with that song."

"That's what my we'eh told me."

"Yes, when you are given a song, you must use it for good things. You will help people with that song. Will you sing it for me?"

Uncle Quill tipped his head very close and Chickadee sang the song into his ear. Quill was quiet for a good bit of the time as the oxcart rolled and bounced over the trail. He hummed the song thoughtfully. Finally, he said it was a good song.

"Nokomis would say that song will last through time."

Chickadee let the pleasure of that thought, and the happiness at the thought of seeing his family, fill him.

"Uncle," he said, "do you have a story for me? Perhaps something else that happened to you when you were a boy? Or perhaps about your naming. Your name Quill is a powerful name. I suppose it was given to you as a young warrior. I suppose that your shot was fine as a quill. Or your arrows were always that sharp. I suppose the enemy feared your sharpness."

Uncle Quill was silent. After a while, he looked at Chickadee, shook his wild hair, and laughed.

"One time," he said, "I thought I was a great hunter. I saw a porcupine up in a tree. I knocked it out of the tree and do you know? That baby porcupine, it fell on me! Quills stuck all over in me. There were quills in my arms. Quills on my head. Quills even on the end of my nose. That is how I got my name!"

"Oh," said Chickadee. He tried not to sound disappointed, but he was surprised.

"I was always playing tricks on people, always teasing your mother. I wasn't a great hero, you know," said Quill.

"Did you save *anybody*?" asked Chickadee. "Did you kill a bear as it charged you?"

"No," said Quill.

"Did a thousand warriors surround you and you terrified them with your war cry?"

"No," said Quill.

"Did you put out a raging fire?"

"Yes, I did that," Quill remembered happily. "I put out a raging fire once! The fire was raging on the seat of my pants. I put it out by dunking my butt in a bucket of water."

"You are so big and strong," said Chickadee, almost desperate now, "you must have done something brave!"

"Not yet," said Quill. "But I did take care of that little namesake, that porcupine. It lived with me for a year. I didn't eat him even when we nearly starved to death."

"That's pretty good," said Chickadee.

"If you want some good hunting stories, you should ask Two Strike."

"I'd be scared to ask Two Strike," said Chickadee.

"Did you ever hear about the time Two Strike rode a moose?"

"No," said Chickadee.

"I'll tell you," said Quill. "One day Two Strike was paddling her canoe on the lake and there she saw a moose, just swimming along in front of her. You know how she always has her knives or her gun for hunting?"

"Always," said Chickadee, who couldn't imagine her otherwise.

"This time she'd forgotten everything. Imagine, she'd just gone out to enjoy the day. This, she never did. And here a moose swims right up to her. Of course, she wanted to hunt that moose."

"Of course," said Chickadee.

"She had only a rope," said Quill. "So she tied that rope around the moose and then jumped out of the boat right onto the moose's back. So there she was, riding on the moose in the lake, just as easy as you please. She steered it by the antlers. Of course, pretty soon the moose wants to get out of the lake, and out he comes. Two Strike is now on top of the moose, riding it like a horse. Do you think the moose likes that?"

"No," said Chickadee.

"Oh, you can bet it doesn't like this one bit! The moose can't see what is on its back, but knows it isn't good. That moose starts running furiously through the woods. It runs under low branches, trying to scrape that thing off its back. Two Strike holds on for dear life. If she falls off, that moose will stomp her with its knife-sharp hooves!"

"What happened?"

"After a long, very long while, the moose starts walking slower and slower. Finally, the moose fell asleep. She tired it out, that Two Strike. That moose was walking in its sleep. Two Strike hopped off, still holding that rope, and the moose kept walking in its sleep. She could lead it anywhere. She led that moose home. Back to camp."

"Really?"

"I saw it! Into camp walks Two Strike with that moose walking right beside her, sleepy and gentle as a puppy. Of course, knowing me, you probably know what I did when I saw her bring that sleeping moose into camp."

"What did you do?" asked Chickadee.

"I shouted, *'Wake up!'*" said Quill. "And boy, did it ever startle awake. That moose looked around, turned its head this way and that as though thinking, *How'd I get here?* Then it rears up and tears through the camp, knocking over the kettles, kicking through the wigwams. It tossed a rack of dried fish into the air. Fish rained down everywhere! It caught a blanket on its antlers and the blanket hung down over its eyes. That moose was twirling around and around in the middle of the camp, blinded. That rope swung by Two Strike. She caught the end of the rope, but it fell off the moose. She was laughing too hard to kill that moose. It just ran off, the blanket flapping off its head. Later on, we found that blanket on the ground. It was all torn up. I guess the moose tried to fight it, just stomped it to pieces. Oh, we never forgot that."

Chickadee laughed, imagining the torn blanket. The trail wound through beautiful woods of tamarack, and over corduroy roads that were made of skinned tamarack poles placed together one after the other. The roads were bone-rattling, but nobody got stuck. If one of the poles broke, the oxcart train stopped and cut a new pole to replace it. That was part of the way of the trail, Uncle Quill explained.

"If something on the trail goes wrong, a tree falls across, a pole breaks, then we fix it. We depend on those who went before us to do the same. Once, I explained this to Nokomis. Know what she said?"

"What?"

"She said that was how the world should work. We should fix what we break in this world for the ones who come next, our children."

TWENTY-FOUR

THE SNAKE NEST

"Uncle, look out!"

The oxcarts ahead were slowly slipping into a coulee, and at the bottom there was a steep incline. The more that went down, the harder it was to get out. Uncle Quill halted the ox just in time.

"Now what do we do?"

"Har!"

It was the brothers, who had taken a great liking to Antoinette's family in the cart just behind. Babiche and Batiste were surveying the difficult mess below, and decided that their bellies were full enough to help push the carts again. Down they went, and in no time the carts

181

that floundered at the bottom were aided by the pushing shoulders of the two strong brothers.

The rest of the train took a circuitous route that took them along a rough, woody trail to avoid the deep, dry streambed. It looped around and soon rejoined the bone-jarringly bumpy road. Chickadee jumped out of the cart and walked beside the ox. Walking was much better. As he accompanied the ox that day, he saw his namesake. The little bird hovered near, then perched on the collar of the ox. It was singing, or saying something, or trying to tell Chickadee some piece of news. The little bird was so intent, trying to communicate. But the wheels of the carts were so loud, Chickadee couldn't hear what his namesake was trying to tell him.

That night, however, Chickadee dreamed of his brother.

Makoons was lying still, drained and quiet. Omakayas sat with him, wiping his face and hands with cool leaves.

"Brother"—his voice was thin—"oh, brother Chickadee. Please help me to live!"

Chickadee woke with a cold chill in his heart, and tears running down the sides of his cheeks. His shirt was damp with the tears he'd cried in his sleep. The camp was quiet. Quill snored softly beside him. The ox was chewing cud beside the cart, dozing on its feet.

"Brother," whispered Chickadee, "I am coming as fast as I can! Wait for me. Just wait for me a little!"

• • •

After Chickadee fell asleep again, he slept peacefully. But just at dawn, he was awakened by screams and laughter throughout the camp. Chickadee sat up and felt something drop off his neck. He brushed gently at his buffalo robe and in the half-light he could see dozens of tiny snakes slip to the ground. Turning to Uncle Quill, who snored happily on his back, he saw that his uncle was completely covered by snakes. There was even a tiny baby snake curled happily on the warm broad plane of Quill's forehead. With every snore, the tiny snake slipped toward Quill's open mouth.

Chickadee reached carefully over and plucked away the snake. Delicately, he took another snake from behind his uncle's ear. There were six curled for warmth on Quill's chest. One poked his head out, and the curious red tongue flickered just beneath his collar. Chickadee took each one off and let it down to the earth gently, then shooed it away. They sped out beneath the flap of the robe, the way they had come in. Chickadee kept on removing snakes from his sleeping uncle until his uncle blinked awake.

"What are you doing?"

"Oh, nothing. Good morning, my uncle," said Chickadee.

Quill yawned and crawled out from under the cart. The shrieks and laughter had subsided. Apparently, in the night, everyone had been visited by snakes. The baby snakes had crawled in with the people because they were warm. The snakes had slipped into peoples' blankets and were sliding all through the camp. They were harmless snakes, black with lovely yellow bellies and clean yellow stripes down their sides. Chickadee had always liked snakes. Probably, he thought, the oxcart train had camped near a huge snake-hatching nest, a place where snakes return each year to lay their eggs. These mysterious places were ancient. Nokomis had once told Chickadee that the snake nests went back to the beginning of time. The original snakes had told the present-day snakes where to go, and they still followed their old traditions.

Quill stretched his arms. His moccasins with the tall red leggings attached stood just behind the wheel, where he'd removed them before turning in to sleep. He lifted one and two snakes writhed to get out.

"Aaaaagggggg! Ginebigoog!" screamed Quill. He hopped around the back of the wheel in terror, then looked around, embarrassed.

"Here, my uncle," said Chickadee, hurrying to grab

the moccasins. He shook them out and then his uncle gingerly put his feet into them.

"Ugh," he shuddered. "Ginebigoog!"

"They are gone now, my uncle," said Chickadee.

"I have always been scared of snakes," said Uncle Quill sheepishly. "I am *so* happy they did not attack me in my sleep or crawl into my blankets! I have powerful snake medicine, though. It keeps them away."

"Yes," said Chickadee, letting one last little snake go into the grass. "Your snake medicine sure worked!"

The rocky and brutal part of the trail seemed to go on forever, but Quill was an expert driver, and he managed to come through without breaking a cart wheel or axle. Now they forded the Leaf River, the bottom pebbly and clear. They traveled up to Otter Tail City, which was only a few cabins and a trading post. The little outpost, which was hardly a city, stood on the northern shore of a lake so beautiful that everyone was glad to camp there. All of the children, including Chickadee, went swimming. The shallow and gentle beaches stretched so far that the water had already warmed. There were no stones to hurt a child's feet. Little fish swam curiously near and nibbled at their toes. The women went out together, holding up the blankets and laughing as they bathed apart from everyone. Afterward, the carts were left up in the shade and everyone made fires and set their tents up on the beaches.

The beach was a lovely pale brown sand, fine as powder in some places. The lake was huge. Chickadee could not see across it, and he couldn't see a single island. The clear water seemed to stretch forever, and the sun went down slowly and spread fire across its western edge.

Chickadee collected white beach wood, and that night he and his uncle made their own fire. Babiche brought down a duck and gave it to Chickadee as a gift. He had even cleaned and plucked it!

"Remember this gift, and tell Two Strike," said Babiche.

Uncle Quill put the duck on a stick over the fire, and while the ox munched beach grass in the trees behind them, they roasted and ate the duck. It was a delicious duck, juicy and tender. Quill had bought some dried cherries at the trading post, and they ate that treat slowly, along with bannock from Antoinette. The two were quiet. Uncle Quill smoked his pipe. They did not speak, just gazed across the water and listened to the musical slap and swish of waves. Chickadee knew that in his heart his uncle missed their own lake, the numberless islands, the beautiful beaches and hidden coves where they had spent so many happy days. As for Chickadee, he could not forget his dream.

"My brother, I am coming," he whispered to the gentle waves.

TWENTY-FIVE

THE WIND

Wㅤhen the wind blew on the plains it was harsher, louder, stronger. There was nothing to stop it. The spring wind pummeled the little cabin where Makoons lay ill again. It tore screeching at the planks of the roof. It squeezed between the chinking of the logs in soft whistles. It moaned through the eaves and hissed through the oil-papered windows. The wind was noisy and constant. The wind agitated Makoons.

"Listen," he sat up. "I hear my brother!"

"No, my boy," Nokomis said, "drink this tea and sleep."

But either Makoons could not sleep, tossing and turning

in his fever, or he did sleep, too much, for days, frightening them all.

"I'm sure I hear him!" cried Makoons.

"Shhh," said Omakayas. There were tears in her eyes.

One afternoon there was a tap on the doorsill. It was Father Belcourt, bringing his cross and a bowl of soup. He set the bowl down beside Makoons.

"This is light on the stomach," he said. He felt Makoons's forehead. "He burns."

"Yes, good father."

"Would you like me to say a prayer?"

"No, good father."

Father Belcourt took a bannock from a sack he carried and laid it beside the soup.

"I will say a prayer on my own and hope for your son's restoration," said Father Belcourt. He made the sign of the cross and ducked out the door. The wind plucked up his cassock and cloak and blew it around his thin shanks in a wild billow.

"He is a good priest," Omakayas said to Animikiins.

"We have our own prayers," said Animikiins. "And I have my father's drum. He said that I should play his song when I needed his help. I need his help now."

Animikiins began to sing and play softly. He requested that the spirits enter the cabin. He asked them to gather around Makoons. He called their names, he called them out of each direction. He called their namesakes, the animals, from each direction. He called their colors. He begged them to come into the cabin and heal his son. As Animikiins sang, he closed his eyes and remembered how his father had come from the spirit world to help him live when he had fallen through the ice. His father had stood there in his blanket covered with his own namesake, the lightning and thunder, and helped his son find the strength to lift himself from the freezing water.

Now, Animikiins sang to his own son, begging him to gather the strength.

"My brother, I hear you!" said Makoons.

Makoons sat up again and stared fixedly at the door. Omakayas began to weep. Fear tore at her heart. It seemed to her that Makoons was talking to his brother in the spirit world. She feared that Chickadee had died after all, and now his spirit was pulling Makoons's spirit along with it to the other side.

"Lie down, my dear boy. Hush," said Omakayas.

She stroked Makoons's arms with a cool wet piece of soft buckskin. She kept the rest of him comfortable and warm in the best blankets they had. She watched over him day and night, rarely taking a rest herself. Nokomis had to force her to sleep. She was afraid that they could lose Omakayas too. All her healing would be for nothing, useless, like that time way back in the beginning of Omakayas's life, when there was smallpox.

That disease had taken Omakayas's little brother, just a

baby. He had died in her arms. Omakayas was determined that she would save her son. This would not happen to Makoons. Yet no matter what she did, he did not improve. He stayed feverish and listless, and now he was hearing strange things.

Yet, who didn't hear strange things with this wind?

Outside, the wind picked up, screaming like a thousand mad fiddles, and getting louder and louder. Omakayas put her hands over her ears. The screeching continued, and got closer. Nokomis held Makoons in her arms, and Animikiins stood up, slowly, in the little cabin. Two Strike was outside with the horses, battling the wind with them in their pole barn. The rest of the family was off gathering more wood for the cart that Mikwam was building. The wind howled with such insane fury that the group inside feared that a tornado might have formed, might be rushing at them. The door shook. The logs seemed to rattle in their sockets.

"My brother is here!" Makoons shouted.

Omakayas's blood ran cold and along with Nokomis she put her arms around him and was about to burst into tears when the door slammed open and in walked Chickadee.

"Brother!"

Both brothers shouted at once, and then there was a collapse of confused feeling. Everyone was hugging everyone. Uncle Quill had come in too, and Animikiins was pounding on his back in joy. Chickadee was in his mother's arms, along with Makoons. They were right where they belonged.

The night was long, the wind still harsh, but Animikiins took his drum out again. This time Chickadee sang the song he had been taught by his namesake. He remembered its healing power, and put every bit of his love and energy into each word. Makoons, very weak, listened with a smile and slowly licked the other half of the peppermint stick. There were bits of dried leaf on the stick, and in places the red coloring had come off. But the flavor made him happy as he listened. He could not get enough of his brother's singing. He would always love the sound of his brother's voice. He asked for his brother's song, over and over. Every time that Chickadee sang the song, Makoons could feel his strength grow inside of him.

"Please, brother, sing," he said.

So Chickadee sang.

I am only the Chickadee
Yet small things have
    great power
I speak the truth.

AUTHOR'S NOTE
ON THE OJIBWE LANGUAGE

Obijbwemowin was originally a spoken, not written, language, and for that reason spellings are often idiosyncratic. There are also many, many dialects in use. To make the Obijbwemowin in the text easier to read, I have sometimes used phonetic spellings. I apologize to the reader for any mistakes and refer those who would like to encounter the language in depth to *A Concise Dictionary of Minnesota Ojibwe*, edited by John D. Nichols and Earl Nyholm; to the *Oshkaabewis Native Journal*, edited by Anton Treuer; and to the curriculum developed by Dennis Jones at the University of Minnesota.

GLOSSARY AND PRONUNCIATION
GUIDE OF OJIBWE TERMS

aadizookaan (ahd-zoh-kahn): a traditional story that often helps explain how to live as an Ojibwe

aadizookaanag (ahd-zoh-khan-ahg): the plural form of **aadizookaan**

ahneen (ah-NEEN): greeting

anama'eminensag (ah-nam-ah'ay-min-ayns-ug): praying berries or ropes

Anishinabe (AH-nish-in-AH-bay): the original name for the Ojibwe or Chippewa people, a Native American group who originated in and live mainly in the northern North American woodlands. There are currently Ojibwe reservations in Michigan, Wisconsin, Minnesota, North Dakota, Ontario, Manitoba, Montana, and Saskatchewan

Anishinabeg (AH-nish-in-AH-bayg): the plural

form of **Anishinabe**

    baka'akwen (bah-kah-ah-kweh-n): chicken

    bezhig (bay-zhig): one

    Biboonang (Bib-oon-ung): Winter Spirit

    bine (bin-ay): partridge

    binewag (bin-ay-wug): the plural form of **bine**

    biwabik (bii-wahb-ick): metal

    bizindaan (bih-zin-dahn): listen

    Bwaan-akiing (Bwahn-ah-keeng): the land of the Dakota and Lakota people, two other Native tribes

    Deydey (DAY-day): Daddy

    dibi' (dih-bih): I don't know where

    eya' (ay-yah): yes

    gaawiin (gah-WEEN): no

    geget (GEH-geht): surely, or for emphasis, truly or really

    gidebwe (ghih-day-bway): you speak the truth

    gigawaabamin (gih-gah-WAH-bah-min): I will see you

    giigawedaa (gee-gah-way-day): let's go home

    giiwedin (gee-way-din): north

    gijigijigaaneshiinh (gih-jih-gih-jih-gah-nay-shee): chickadee

    ginebigoog (ghin-ay-big-oog): snakes

    Gizhe Manidoo (Gih-zhay Man-ih-do): the great, kind spirit

    gookoosh (goo-koosh): pig

howaa (HOW-ah): a sound of approval

Iskigamizige-giizis (Iss-kay-gah-mih-zih-gey-giizis): April

majaan (mah-jahn): go away!

makak (mah-KUK): a container of birchbark folded and often stitched together with basswood fiber. Ojibwe people use these containers today, especially for traditional feasts

makakoon (mah-kah-koon): the plural form of **makak**

manoomin (mah-NOH-min): wild rice; the word means "the good seed"

mashi (mahsh-ih): yet

mashkiig (maash-keeg): swampy place

mekadewikonyewinini (meh-kah-day-wih-kone-iy-eh-in-in-ih): black robe/priest

memegwesiwag (may-may-gway-see-wug): the plural form of **memegwesi**, little people

miigwech (mee-gwetch): thank you

minopogwad (min-oh-poh-gwud): it tastes good

naanan (nahn-an): five

nashke (nahsh-kay): look

niiwin (nee-win): four

niizh (neezh): two

nimama (nee-mama): my mama

niswi (niss-way): three

Nokomis (no-KOH-mis): grandmother

Nookoo (Noo-koo): shortened version of **Nokomis**
waabooz (WAH-booz): rabbit
we'eh (way-ay): namesake
wigwam (WIHG-wahm): a birchbark house
wigwassi-wigamig (wig-wass-ih-wig-ahm-ig): house
Zhawanong (Zhah-wah-nung): the South